GINGER DANGER

MINT CHOCOLATE CHIP MYSTERIES, BOOK 2

EMMIE LYN

© 2020, Emmie Lyn

All rights reserved. Except as permitted under the U.S. Copyright Act of 1976, no part of this publication may be reproduced, distributed or transmitted in any form or by any means, or stored in a database or retrieval system without the prior written permission of the publisher.

Editor: Helen Page
Proofreader: Alice Shepherd
Cover Designer: Lou Harper, Cover Affairs

This is a work of fiction. Names, characters, organizations, places, events, and incidents are either products of the author's imagination or are used fictitiously. Any resemblance to actual persons, living or dead, or actual events is purely coincidental.

No part of this work may be reproduced, or stored in a retrieval system, or transmitted in any form or by any means, electronic, mechanical, photocopying, recording, or otherwise, without written permission of the publisher.

Sweet Promise press
PO Box 72
Brighton, MI 48116

To every cozy mystery reader, a heartfelt thank you. You make it all worth it!

ABOUT THIS BOOK

It's no secret that, I, Sunny Shaw, am a magnet for mayhem right here on beautiful Blueberry Bay.

So, when a woman goes missing just before the grand opening of Shakes and Cakes, I think...it could be worse. And of course that's exactly what happens when missing turns into dead. It's hard to cry over a disastrous opening when there's a murderer running around and things aren't about to get any easier!

Oh my, Jasper, how will we ever juggle my nasty neighbor, a stalker, a murderer, finding homes for kittens AND serving the best shakes and cakes in Pineville?

The answer to that million dollar question might save my business but can we shake things up to keep my friends out of jail and me alive to see another day?

AUTHOR'S NOTE

Hi cozy readers!

Welcome to Pineville on Blueberry Bay on the coast of Maine where cozy mysteries abound. If you've read the Little Dog Diner Cozy Mystery series, you've already met Sunny Shaw and her lovable Newfoundland mix, Jasper. Sunny and Jasper are front and center in the Mint Chocolate Chip Mystery series. Sit back and enjoy. But beware... you're about to fall in love with adorable kittens, be tempted by tasty shakes, and delicious sweets while each story in this exciting series brings you on a twisty turny mystery!

[Click here to sign up for my newsletter and never miss a new release.](#)

1

I hadn't slept a wink.

What was that all about? Normally, I, Sunny Shaw, hours away from becoming Pineville, Maine's newest business owner, slept like the dead through almost anything. Yet, I'd tossed and turned all night.

I couldn't blame my anxiety on Jasper, my giant Newfoundland mix. With a name like Jasper, people always assumed she was a male but I decided, if the name fit, wear it. Proudly. And she did.

Anyway, usually she'd give me gentle nudges to get me out of bed when she wanted food or a trip outside, but her snores and snuffles told me she was still dreaming of chasing rabbits. My two kittens, Stash and Princess Muffin, usually started their day practicing head pounces to get me to fill their food bowls. So far, though, they hadn't moved from the bottom of the bed where they'd each carved out a spot last night and fallen fast asleep. Not even the sun rising over Blueberry Bay had yet to peep through my window on this glorious late-summer Maine morning. And worst of all, when I looked at my bedside clock at regular, two-minute intervals, I'd swear it was standing still.

The reason for my restlessness all night? Excitement mixed with worry. Today was the day. Would my dream come true or sink like a lobster boat hitting a rock?

Was Ty Hitchner losing any sleep? He was my friend, business partner, and well, I'll leave it at that for now. He and I had put our money, hard work, and future on the line with a new business venture —the Shakes and Cakes Shop. The grand opening, scheduled for a few short hours from now, accounted for my frazzled nerves and lack of sleep.

My head buzzed with questions. Would we have any customers? Would our Kitty Castle for stray cats and kittens attached to the rear of the shop be a success? Would Hitch and I be able to work well together? Gad... I felt like pulling my hair out.

I tried to tell myself that just because something

could go wrong, didn't mean it would. However, much as I tried to focus on the positive, I still obsessed over that possibility.

I sighed, slipped my feet from under the sheet and padded to the shower. The best remedy for this waiting game was to get on with it. If I got up early, I had extra time to get ready for this important day.

After the steamy hot water had me fully awake, I pulled my dark hair into a French braid, slipped on my new white t-shirt, and stepped into my dark blue skinny jeans. I twisted from one side to the other and checked out how I looked in my full-length mirror. My blue eyes reflected back at me with an encouraging, you-can-do-this expression. I gave myself two thumbs up, my ensemble perfect for serving thick shakes, healthy smoothies, and a variety of donuts and cakes to the line of customers we hoped would stream in today.

Correction... that *would* stream in.

My last addition to my look was to clasp on my favorite good luck necklace. The gold sun pendant, a gift from my friend who'd been murdered on his boat several months ago. I rubbed the smooth sun, remembering Benny's warm friendship. I hoped he was rooting for my new endeavor.

I snapped my fingers, feeling much better about

the day. "Come on Jasper. It's time to get this show on the road."

Urgent knocking on my front door got me rushing downstairs, and Jasper's barks, loud enough to shake my house, sent the kittens scrambling for cover under the couch in my small living room.

My day had officially begun.

"Sunny? Open up. I've got coffee and a bag of cinnamon and sugar donut holes."

Well, this was a bright beginning—my favorite surprise treat personally delivered by Hitch. My heart always beat a little faster when he was around.

I pulled the door open and grabbed the bag from him, inhaling the sweet scent and groaning with anticipation.

"Good morning to you, too, Sunshine." He patted my head like I was an annoying little sister as he walked inside. Yeah, we'd been friends for a long time and once, I'd hoped that friendship would turn into something else. For now, being friends and business partners with Hitch was challenge enough. At least that's what I told myself.

Before I closed the door, my neighbor, Tilly, hollered, "Wait for me." She waved as she hurried across the street in her chili pepper-red jogging outfit. She'd probably been sitting in her rocking chair for hours, with her big orange cat, Pinky, waiting for activity to start at my house.

Tilly was my surrogate grandmother, without the sweet old lady part. She loved attention, action, and getting into trouble. Translation? She was more often than not, a bad influence.

"Finally," she said when she walked in, giving Hitch a little peck on his cheek. "I thought you two would never get started today. Isn't this your grand opening?"

"Yup." He handed her a coffee. Of course, he'd planned ahead and brought three. Then, he checked me out from head to toe. "And, I'm glad to see that Sunny's dressed and ready to go. I thought I'd have to pull her out of bed. Nice look, too."

His compliment pleased me more than it should have, but since I never knew if he was teasing or flirting, I punched his arm.

"Ha ha," I said. I couldn't take my eyes off his brand-new jeans that fit perfectly. He rocked them with a snug green t-shirt that matched his eyes. I wondered if he planned it that way or just lucked into the winning combination.

"I thought you weren't coming until seven and it's," I looked at my clock just as it chimed its half hour song, "only six-thirty."

I popped a donut hole in my mouth and handed the bag back to Hitch, mumbling, "Don't let Tilly eat them all while I take Jasper for a walk around the block."

"I'll come with you," he said.

"Fine," Tilly grabbed the bag away from Hitch and peered inside. "I hope you brought some glazed ones, too. You know I don't like cinnamon and sugar."

"Yes, I know, Tilly." Hitch took my elbow and steered me to the sidewalk, not that I needed any steering with Jasper's hundred and fifty or so pounds pulling me along until we reached my neighbor's flower garden.

"Jasper. Keep going." Now, it was my turn to tug on the leash, but she outweighed me by at least thirty pounds. If she wanted to stop and sniff the edge of the garden, that's exactly what she'd do. I glanced at the front windows for any movement but saw nothing.

My neighbor, Violet, wasn't crazy about me and usually had her eagle eyes watching for an excuse to complain about Jasper. Finally, my Newfie trotted forward without trampling any zinnias, and I sighed with relief.

Hitch flung his arms to the side and breathed in

deeply. "Nothing like fresh morning air to clear out all the worries. How'd you sleep?"

"Not a wink. You?"

"Too excited to sleep. Everything's all set. It's do or die today. We'll find out what the good people in Pineville think about our crazy Shakes and Cakes Shop."

"That's the problem, Hitch. What if it bombs?" The butterflies I'd been trying to calm down in my stomach, all decided to take off at the same time. Good thing I'd only eaten one donut hole, or I'd be embarrassing myself at the edge of the sidewalk.

Hitch casually draped his arm over my shoulders as he shortened his pace to match mine. "What if it's such a success we have to put on an addition and hire more help?"

I looked up at him and quirked an eyebrow. "Is that why our partnership works? You balance my worries. Thanks. Your scenario is immensely better than mine."

We turned onto the wooded path that looped behind my house, and I let Jasper's leash drag on the ground. "Speaking of help. I'm kind of worried about having Tilly serve customers. Will she follow the recipes I've made? I'm afraid she'll wing it and mess it all up."

"You know as well as I do that Tilly is Tilly. It's too late now to tell her she can't help, so we'll have to cross our fingers and keep a close eye on her."

My neighbor was all over the idea for a sweet shop and kitty castle and adoption room at the back. Without waiting for an invitation, she signed up to help before the ink was dry on all the legal documents. There were pros and cons to having Tilly work for us even as a volunteer. Today I could only think of the cons.

"Ha. It was *never* an option to tell Tilly she couldn't help. But, cross our fingers? *That's* reassuring." I picked up Jasper's leash as we turned the last corner, back toward my house.

Hitch pulled me to a stop and faced me. "It's okay to be nervous. Just don't obsess about all that might go wrong, Sunny. Focus on the positives. The Kitty Castle in the greenhouse is the most fantastic idea you've ever had."

I smiled at his praise and agreed one hundred percent. We'd created, with the help of Conrad Coleman, an environment filled with tropical plants, climbing structures, and cozy sleeping spots that the family of cats we'd found would love. We were starting off with the stray kittens and their mama cat, but they would most likely only be the beginning. I was proud of how it had all come together.

"After the customers buy their shakes and wander into the greenhouse to find a table, the orchid plants in bloom, pots of herbs, and tropical vines will wow them. Right?" he said.

I nodded.

"And then, they'll see all those magical fluff balls that have a temporary home in the jungle. They're irresistible, Sunny, and you'll cry every time one gets adopted."

He was right, but they'd be happy tears. As much as I loved each and every one of those kittens, they needed a forever home. I also knew that as soon as one was adopted, more would show up needing my help. Cats had a nose for a softy like me who'd provide free room and board.

"There's Tilly," Hitch said, pulling me away from my thoughts. "She must have gone home to change. She's dressed to kill in her I-can-look-like-a-grownup skirt and white linen tunic. And she's even wearing her bright pink scarf. I guess she means business today."

Jasper pulled us toward home, and I said a silent prayer that Tilly was on her best behavior.

I could always hope, I told myself.

2

Hitch and I drove over to our Shakes and Cakes Shop together in his blue Camaro. Jasper squeezed in the back and slobbered all over the window until Hitch rolled it down a crack and she stuck her nose out to sniff the crisp morning air. I hoped we'd left in plenty of time to check, double-check, and check once more that everything was in order before we hung up the *open* flag.

As we drove through Pineville, I pictured our business finally opening up to the public after months of planning and preparation. Had we overlooked anything? The brick path winding under an arch led customers through a riot of blooms in pots and gardens. Our bee balm, phlox, petunias, and begonias perfumed the air until they reached the building covered with aged cedar shakes. Everything melded into a stunning and inviting setting.

Tilly had insisted on meeting us there. She loved her new chili pepper red convertible Volkswagen beetle and was sure to make a flashy grand entrance.

"Are you nervous?" I asked Hitch as I studied his profile framed by his longish light brown hair. One thing he'd perfected in the years I'd known him was hiding his emotions. Based on the set of his jaw, relaxed as if he were enjoying a private joke, I'd assume this whole venture we were about to embark on was no big deal to him.

"A little," he said, glancing in my direction and rewarding me with one of his genuine smiles that I know came from his heart. "Nervous might not be the right word. Excited describes it better." He reached over and patted my thigh. "I never said it would be easy, Sunny. But I do believe that if we stay focused and work hard, we'll be successful. Like I told you before, the Kitty Castle will pique everyone's curiosity and who can resist a delicious shake and sweet cake once they come through the door?"

"I'm so glad we decided to get our cupcakes from the Little Dog Diner and donuts from A Donut A Day, at least for now. Once we get some cash flow, we should think about adding someone who can do all that in-house. What do you think?"

"And that day will come sooner rather than later," he predicted.

We'd reached downtown Pineville, the smallest of the towns clustered along scenic Blueberry Bay. We passed the coffee shop, hardware store, and A Donut A Day. The library and police station were just off the main street.

My heart raced when our brand new Shakes and Cakes Shop sign came into view. A crazy shake covered with blue-tinted whipped cream was our nod to Blueberry Bay.

Hitch slowed down. "Ready for this, Sunshine?" he asked before he pulled into *our* parking lot.

I nodded. Of course, I was.

In the next moment I did a double-take. What was a big silver SUV with New York license plate doing parked right in front of our potted plant display?

"Who is that?" I said, glaring at a vehicle I'd never seen before blocking the walkway to Shakes and Cakes.

Before Hitch had a chance to answer, the driver door opened and a long, slender leg appeared. When the rest of the body emerged from the car, it was attached to a woman who wiggled and adjusted and patted her tight skirt into place.

Hitch gasped. "What's *she* doing here?"

"You know her?" I'd never seen this red-haired beauty in my life. She looked around our premises and wrinkled her nose as if our business was beneath her dignity.

My body tensed, flooding me once again, with angst. It was just the attitude I'd feared from the public.

Hitch's gaze stayed on the intruder. "Yeah, I know her, and I've got a bad feeling. But, don't worry, Sunny, I'll get rid of her. Take Jasper and go ahead inside and check on the kittens."

Go inside? Not on your life, Hitch. He couldn't ditch me that easily. I wasn't going to miss finding out what this was all about first-hand. "What's her name?"

"Ginger Ross," he said with a look that said just saying her name tasted like a stale moldy donut.

"Come on Jasper." I opened the door so she could squeeze out of the back of the Camaro. If my guess was right, Ms. Ginger Ross was not going to be pleased when Jasper gave her a hearty welcome. I laughed to myself at the image of black Newfoundland hairs on that fancy dark green skirt or silky cream blouse.

It went better than I expected because Jasper beat Hitch to our visitor. She gave a friendly woof but to the untrained ear, it sounded more like a foghorn. Jasper followed it up with one of her enthusiastic greetings. Threads of drool flew through the air and landed on our haughty visitor's skirt, leaving dark lines of wet slobber from the waistline to the hem.

Ginger pinched her lips together.

I covered my laugh.

And, right on time, Tilly, top down and radio blaring, screeched to a stop next to Hitch's car, sending a cloud of dust blowing Ginger's way. The look on her face as she flicked particles of Shakes and Cakes fine gravel off her blouse said it all with one glare at Tilly—anger, disgust, and maybe a touch of hatred.

Ginger marched to Tilly's car, yanked her door open and stared at her over the steering wheel. "You're a menace. You shouldn't have a license."

Tilly slowly pushed the scarf off her gray hair, adjusted her sunglasses, and looked up at Ginger. "And you are?"

"Ginger Ross," she said as if we should all bow

down like she was royalty or something. "I'm here to talk to Hitch."

"Well, la-di-diddly-da," Tilly said and held her hand toward Ginger, obviously asking for assistance getting out of her car. Of course, Ginger had no way of knowing that Tilly was far from a feeble old lady. Puzzled but polite, Ginger leaned forward to help Tilly, who accidentally, on purpose I think, tripped, sending the coffee in her open cup right onto the front of Ginger's outfit. Well, at least now she matched with dark stains on her silky blouse *and* her slobbery skirt.

A snort snuck out. I know it wasn't the proper thing to do, but the expression of complete shock on Ginger's face sent me over the edge and I lost any possibility of control.

Tilly pulled a cotton handkerchief out of her skirt pocket and dabbed at the stain on Ginger's blouse. "I'm so sorry. You're so much stronger than I expected and well, silly Tilly, I lost my balance."

Ginger said nothing. What could she say in a situation like that? Not much. Instead, she marched to Hitch. "We need to talk."

"Why are you here, Ginger?" It looked like Hitch was forcing a straight face without much luck.

"That's a good question. I wish I'd never had the

crazy idea to meet up with my college roommates this weekend. And here of all places in this... this village. There isn't even a gas station here. And, I can't find my friend's house."

Yeah, and that giant tank of hers probably eats more gas than a fleet of Tilly's Volkswagens, I said to myself.

"You have a friend?" Hitch asked, receiving another glare from Ginger. If she didn't watch out, her face would be etched with frown wrinkles that even regular Botox treatments wouldn't be able to erase. "I mean, you have a friend here in Pineville?"

"I do. Violet Burnham. She lives on Cobbler Lane."

My heart sank. That was my neighbor. Now, I'd have to deal with someone out to get Jasper in trouble *plus* this New York woman with an oversized attitude.

"How did you know where to find *me*?" Hitch was as puzzled as I was about that little detail.

"Conrad told me you had some kind of grand opening today." She looked around again. "Is this it?"

I hoped this wasn't an indication for how the rest of the day would go.

3

"Yes Ginger, this *is* our grand opening. But we're too busy to help you now," Hitch said. Without another word, he took me by my arm and headed toward our front door where Jasper paced impatiently.

"You're just going to brush me off like that?"

My back was to Ginger, but from her tone, I'm sure she even stamped her foot in the dirt.

"Yup," Hitch answered and opened the door to our shop, stepped aside, and held his hand out for me to enter ahead of him. What a gentleman. At least to me.

"I'll be back," she said getting in the last word. I heard her car door close with a loud thud and she drove off.

"What the heck was that all about?" Tilly asked when she'd caught up with us. I had to hand it to her, she didn't have a drop of coffee on her mid-calf skirt or white tunic. What aim, and at her age.

Hitch ran his fingers through his hair, showing a moment of frustration. "I wish I knew. She was Harry's friend. You remember? The guy I worked for in New York. Apparently, she met Conrad through Harry, too. I didn't really know her except that she was someone I didn't want to cross. I'd heard that she holds a grudge and always gets even."

Great. Just the kind of person we needed in our life. Not!

Fortunately, I didn't have time to obsess about Ginger Ross. I was busy assessing the look of the shop. The gleaming oak counter where customers would line up to order from our fabulous menu of fruity, frosty shakes and treats, the several counter stools, and round tables and chairs set up to give a view of the lush garden artfully arranged with both familiar and exotic plants and flowers.

Jasper had pushed her way into the greenhouse and let out a loud woof. Her way of asking me to open the inner door so she could check on her kitty friends. As Chief Kitty Nanny, she had an important job to do, and she took it seriously.

I gave her a scratch to thank her for her, ahem, attention to Ms. Ross and said, "Sorry for the delay, Jasper. I'm glad you manage to quickly deal with unnecessary distractions and keep everything in the right perspective."

I opened the screen door into our greenhouse jungle of vines, towering ponytail palms, and blooming bird of paradise plants carefully placed among Hitch's orchid collection. I hit the control to open the roof vents and turned on the fans to circulate cooler fresh air throughout the greenhouse. After a quick count of the kitties—four plus Mama Cat—I left Jasper lying in the shade of a rubber tree with kittens pouncing on her tail. Time to return to the Shakes and Cakes Shop, conveniently attached only feet away from the greenhouse.

Tilly was busy filling the glass pastry case with iced cupcakes, giant cookies, and sweet donuts. I did spot one hole in the middle of the glazed donut selection where Tilly had decided to eat her pay. No problem.

The door jingled, and I looked up from tucking chairs under tables, surprised to see Conrad Coleman walk in. He'd done the remodeling for us, so it made sense that he'd show up, but he'd told me that he was busy and wouldn't have time to stop in until later in the day.

"All set?" he asked, looking around and nodding with satisfaction at our colorful décor of bright blue chair pads, sunshine yellow tablecloths, and burnt orange napkins. I loved how the interior popped with colors that matched our gardens outside. "This looks great," he said, pointing to the long blackboard on the wall behind the counter listing our special shakes for the day and what we hoped would become our standard favorites.

I looped an apron over my head and tied it in back. Somewhere, Tilly had found just enough hot pink aprons covered with colorful milkshakes for each of us. I hadn't been sure that Hitch would wear one, but I spotted the hot pink ruffled number tied around his waist as he pulled out ingredients from the fridge for our crazy shakes and breakfast smoothies.

"I think so," I said to Conrad. I didn't really have time for this question, but I asked anyway. "What can you tell me about a Ginger Ross?"

He rolled his eyes. "Did she show up here already? I told her your grand opening is today. I can't believe she didn't wait until you weren't so busy. But, that's Ginger. She thinks the sun rises and sets on her impulses. She wants what she wants and has no patience or consideration for anyone else's schedule."

"Do you know why she wants to talk to Hitch?"

Conrad, mid-forties, muscular, and hardly a shrinking violet, shuffled his feet awkwardly. "She told me that she thinks someone is stalking her." He shrugged like he thought this was one of Ginger's weird ideas. "She wants to hire Hitch as her bodyguard."

"That's crazy," I said. "Hitch won't agree to that. We've got this business to run."

I peeked to check that Hitch was still busy behind the counter and lowered my voice so he wouldn't hear us. I wanted to get the whole story first before he got the news.

"I'm sure you're right but Ginger can be persuasive. She's prepared to pay him whatever it takes for his services. Anyway, I see you've got all kinds of shakes and smoothies on your blackboard. Any chance I could get something before the rush is on?"

I'm sure my eyes lit up. Our first customer. "Sure thing, Conrad," I said. "What would you like to try or do you want me to surprise you?"

A smile curled the edges of his mouth and he said, "I'm not real fond of surprises, especially when it's food." He tapped his lips while he studied our menu. "That maple oat coffee combo sounds like it will give me the caffeine kick I need."

"Do you want a scoop of vanilla ice cream in it or the healthy version?" I raised my eyebrows teasing him with a delicious option.

He chuckled and said, "I wish you hadn't given me a choice like that. Ice cream in the morning isn't usually on my menu, but... hey, what the heck. You only live once, right?"

I laughed. "Great choice. Tell Tilly. She'll blend it up for you." I cupped my hand around my mouth and whispered again, "She needs a few practice runs before we open for business."

He feigned a frown. "So, now I'm your guinea pig? I'm not sure I like the sound of *that*." He nudged my arm. "Just kidding. Glad to help." He walked to the gleaming oak counter, freshly sanded and shiny with a thick coat of finish. "Mornin' Tilly. Sunny said you're the chief smoothie maker."

Tilly rewarded him with one of her dazzling smiles she reserved for special friends. "She did, did she? I think she's just trying to get out of some hard work. What can I get for you, Conrad?"

While Conrad gave his order, I joined Hitch in the tiny space behind the counter we jokingly called a kitchen. He was slicing strawberries and oranges for fruit smoothies, so I picked up a knife and chopped kale and spinach for green smoothies. We'd decided that the early morning orders would probably be for joggers and folks on their way to work looking for a healthy smoothie and the shakes would be popular later in the day, but we had to be prepared for anything.

"Conrad told me that Ginger wants to hire you," I told Hitch.

"Hire me? For what?"

"She thinks someone is stalking her."

He shrugged. "Not interested." He scooped up the orange slices and put them in a reusable bag, adding it to the other prepared fruit in the fridge.

"She's willing to pay a lot," I said. If Hitch was going to be even a little bit tempted, I wanted to know now instead of getting hit with a surprise when our business was up and running and I really depended on him.

His knife flew over the fruit like a master chef showing off for a commercial.

"Still not interested, Sunny." When I didn't respond, he crossed his arms and stared down at me with those green orbs he has for eyes.

"Do you think I'll do anything if the price is

right? I'm *done* with that kind of job." He raised his arm. The one that took a bullet. "Did you forget the price I paid during my last stint in New York? I got lucky, and my arm is finally one hundred percent healed. And, I don't need her money."

"Thanks, Hitch." I downplayed my tremendous relief. "I told Conrad you wouldn't take the job, but I needed to hear it from you."

A siren pierced the air, growing louder and louder like it was heading right toward our Shakes and Cakes Shop.

"What?" I looked at Hitch feeling unsettled.

Together, we rushed to the front window with a view of the road beyond all the flowers, only to see a Pineville Police cruiser turn into our parking lot.

I looked at Hitch. "I don't like this."

My earlier relief vanished in a flash.

That hadn't lasted for long.

4

Officer Mick Walker jumped out of the driver side of the cruiser, not slowing down to wait for Police Chief Bullock to slide from the passenger seat.

Mick barged into our shop, letting the door slam closed behind him. As he quickly scanned our new shop, his ever-present toothpick bobbed furiously at the edge of his mouth. "I need to talk to everyone here."

The older Police Chief, slightly stooped, limped in behind Mick. He took off his hat and ran his hand over his thinning gray hair. "*I'll* handle this, Officer Walker," he said with authority.

Mick clamped his jaw muscles, biting right through his toothpick, sending it sailing to the floor.

It was no secret that he wanted Chief Bullock to retire. What else everyone suspected, except Mick, was that he wouldn't be the one promoted to Police Chief. He'd pushed the boundaries of his job too many times creating ill-will in Pineville.

I was surprised he even still had a job as an officer on the police force. I, for one, wouldn't shed a tear if he lost his job. The way he hounded Hitch trying to catch him in an infraction made me see red. He'd made it known he had a crush on me, and he saw Hitch as his competition. His bad jokes and self-important manner could *never* win me over.

"We have a situation in town," the Chief said. He eased himself with a painful grimace onto one of the chairs at a round table for two. "A woman visiting Pineville seems to have disappeared. It's still early, and there could very well be a logical explanation, but the last place she was known to be," he paused and looked at each of us in turn, "was here."

"Ginger Ross?" I blurted out accidentally before I covered my mouth with my hand. When I looked at Hitch, he kept a serious poker face, revealing nothing.

"She did stop in, but we weren't open yet," Tilly said, handing Conrad his smoothie. "How about a refreshing smoothie for you, Chief? I can whip up a nice healthy green pick-me-up with kale, bananas, and yogurt. It'll take the edge off that arthritis that looks to be flaring up."

"Will it really help?" he asked, rubbing his hip. He wasn't born yesterday, and his skepticism was obvious.

"It can't hurt." Tilly dumped ingredients into the blender, not measuring anything and whipped the mess together.

"We can't run a business like that, Hitch," I whispered. "She might make someone sick."

"Or kill them." Hitch's lips twitched at the edges with that comment, not that it was funny, but I knew what he meant.

He always tried to lighten the mood, but sometimes his words were just the wrong choice. "Not helpful, Hitch."

I walked over and sat at the table with the Police Chief. My goal? Answer his questions and get him on his way before we opened for business. "Ginger Ross *was* here but she left at least a half hour ago."

"What was she doing here?" he asked accepting the glass of smoothie from Tilly. He smelled it and took a sip through the straw. "Not bad, I suppose," he said, wrinkling his nose. "If you're an herbivore.

With this color, I'm surprised it doesn't taste like mold."

Not exactly the endorsement we needed. This wasn't going well. I had to get Chief Bullock out of here and steer him away from Hitch in the process. "Ginger said she was staying with Violet Burnham on Cobbler Lane. Have you checked with her?"

"Actually, Sunny." He slid the smoothie aside and gave me his full attention. "Violet's the person who called us in a panic. She said this Ginger woman never showed up when she was supposed to. Now, you and I both know how Violet gets a little dramatic at times, so I'm taking her concern with a grain of salt. *But*, at the same time, it's always a good rule to ask a few questions to be on the safe side."

I couldn't argue with his logic, but I also sensed there was a whole lot more behind his words. And, *that* made me squirm.

He set his glass on the table. "Not sure I'll finish that, Tilly. But thanks just the same." One thing I could say about the Police Chief, he was polite, unlike Officer Walker.

"What was she doing here?" Officer Walker demanded to know as he took a step closer, rudely inserting himself into the conversation. "You forgot to answer *that* question, Sunny."

Hitch stood behind me and put his hands on my shoulders, squeezing gently. I saw his game face in his reflection in the window. It helped to reassure me during this moment of uncertainty. "Ginger showed up out of the blue and said she wanted to talk to me." He shrugged like it wasn't any big deal. "I told her I didn't have time because we were busy getting ready for our grand opening. So, she left."

"That's right," Tilly said. "She hopped right back in that big old SUV and screeched out like she was in a rush to go bother someone else."

The Police Chief pushed himself up from his chair. "The funny thing that I can't figure out is why did she come here to talk to you in the first place, Hitch?" He tried to soften the question with a concerned look, but it didn't fool me.

"You'll have to ask Ginger," he said, adding a slight shrug to his answer.

"Which gets us right back to where we started. I need to find this Ginger Ross to ask her that question, don't I? Mind if I have a look around your place?" The Police Chief directed his question toward Hitch like it was a challenge.

"Go right ahead," Hitch said, spreading his arms out to show he had nothing to hide.

"Come on, Walker," the Chief said. Mick bristled.

I chuckled because it sounded like he was calling his dog to tag along. "We'll start in the parking lot."

Mick threw a glare in Hitch's direction, opened his mouth, but closed it quickly. Apparently, he'd experienced a rare moment of restraint. He followed the Police Chief outside and, again, let the door slam.

"Geesh," Tilly said. "What's with all this drama when we don't have time for it?" She picked up the Police Chief's barely tasted smoothie, got a new straw and took a sip, spitting the mouthful back into the glass. "Oh, my goodness, he was right. This is terrible. I guess I overdid the kale."

Conrad, positioned off to one side, had been quiet throughout the ordeal. "From my experience," he said pointedly, "Ginger Ross is nothing but trouble. I'd avoid her at all costs." He sipped through his straw. The gurgling sound indicated he was sucking up every last drop. "Tilly, the smoothie you whipped up for me is delicious. One out of two's not bad."

Actually, we needed every smoothie and milkshake to taste delicious or we'd be sunk before we even began.

But then again, with the arrival and disappearance of Ginger Ross, I might have bigger problems to worry about than the taste of our smoothies.

5

I tried my hardest to get Chief Bullock and Officer Walker out of my thoughts. But I had to wonder what they were looking for as they tromped around our parking lot. I had no clue. We kept glancing outside, proving their presence distressed us all.

Tilly untied her apron and threw it on the counter. "I'm going out there. We open in a half hour and we need them gone."

"Wait." I tried to grab her arm, but she scooted by and was out the door before I could catch her. "This won't end well," I said to Hitch. "In a situation like this, Tilly's filter is off."

"I think her filter is always off," he said. That did

not make me feel better. "She's right, though. Maybe it's better that *she's* pushing them along instead of one of us. We have to look like we aren't hiding anything."

"We aren't, Hitch. At least *I'm* not. Is there something you haven't told me?"

He glanced at Conrad.

"Ginger—"

"What Hitch is trying to say," Conrad interrupted, "is that Ginger had a thing for Hitch, but Hitch brushed her off."

"She's at least ten years older than you," I said, flabbergasted. Of course, as soon as the words were out of my mouth, I realized that age made no difference in matters of the heart. I took a deep breath, calming myself. "How did you let her know you weren't interested?"

"With someone like Ginger, there's no good way to deliver that kind of message. She doesn't take no for an answer," Hitch said. The normal twinkle in his eyes had dulled, and he slumped against the counter. "She told me she always gets what she wants... one way or another. But I never for one second expected her to show up here in Pineville, Sunny. I thought I'd dodged a virtual bullet when I left New York. And to be honest? Actually, getting a bullet in my arm was a whole lot easier to handle than Ginger's stalking."

He rubbed his arm, which had healed, but from the anxious look in his sea green eyes, it must still bring back dark memories.

"But she told Conrad that she came here to hire *you* to protect *her* from a stalker?" I shook my head, totally confused with this conversation.

"She likes to play games," Hitch said, shaking his head as if to rid it of a bad memory. "I think it was her way of letting me know she wouldn't give up."

"Or," Conrad said, "Ginger could have her own stalker, but it would be a hard sell to believe *that* after the number she did on Hitch. And now that she showed up in Pineville, who knows what story she told her friend, Violet. How well do you know her, Sunny?"

A shiver went up my spine when I thought of my irritating neighbor. "I avoid Violet like the plague."

Conrad scratched his head. "That's quite the endorsement. What's her problem?"

"It's more like what *isn't* the problem. She complains every chance she can about Jasper and even makes stuff up. For instance, she says Jasper barks too much, she tramples her flowers, uses her yard as a bathroom, and on and on. All lies. Of course, Jasper barks, but no more than any dog. She's never gone in Violet's yard except for once when Jasper stepped off the sidewalk and did crush a tulip. But the petals were about to fall off anyway." I felt my blood pressure rise just thinking about how much trouble Violet caused. I was on edge every time I took Jasper out.

"I wonder what the connection Ginger and Violet have," Hitch said. "They couldn't be more different except for maybe the not liking Jasper part."

I'd been watching out the window while we talked. Tilly, standing next to her brand new bug, jabbed her finger in Officer Walker's chest. Not good. "Something's happening outside," I said and rushed to the door.

I opened it just in time to hear Tilly say, "She must have dropped it when she helped me out of my car."

Dropped what?

"When a woman drops her pocketbook. she comes right back looking for it," Mick said like he'd just caught Tilly in a trap. He was holding a handbag in his hand and stuffing a few things back inside. I guess he had discovered the identity of the owner.

He had a point about women and their bags, especially someone like Ginger Ross. And someone who most likely paid a fortune for that sleek leather purse.

Tilly shrugged at Mick's comment. She shielded her eyes from the rising morning sun as she looked up at him and said, "So, maybe she'll be back when she discovers it's missing. Like I told you before, she left in a huff. She must have had something on her mind." She reached for the black leather bag. "I'll keep it safe inside behind the counter for her."

Mick laughed and tucked it under his arm. "Nice try. Ginger didn't just happen to drop it, Tilly. The strap is broken. I wonder how *that* happened." He leaned down so he was eye to eye with Tilly. She didn't back off; Tilly thrived on confrontations. "Did you attack her?"

Tilly burst out laughing. "Are you serious? I'm an old lady, Officer Walker. Why would I attack someone I only met this morning?"

Mick picked a toothpick out of his shirt pocket and stuck it in the corner of his mouth, staring Tilly down before he said, "Why indeed? Don't worry, I *will* get to the bottom of this and I don't think I've seen the last of you or your friends about this matter. In case Ginger does return looking for her pocketbook, tell her it's safe and sound… at the police station."

The Police Chief limped around the side of the building. "Sunny? I found this around back." He held up a basket. I peeked in and saw the cutest, fluffiest orange kitty I'd ever seen, eyes closed, and tail wrapped around her body.

"Did one of yours escape?"

"I haven't seen this kitten before," I said taking the basket and setting it in the shade under the awning. "I'll take care of her in a minute." I touched his arm. "Did you find anything interesting in Ginger's pocketbook yet? Like important information about her whereabouts."

His forehead wrinkled. "What are you talking about?"

"Officer Walker found a pocketbook he said belongs to Ginger Ross. You didn't know?"

"Walker! What's that you have?" he shouted, his face red with anger.

"Nothing, Sir."

"Well, let me see what you're holding, and *I'll*

decide if it's nothing. Bring it over here," he ordered in a voice that made his irritation clear.

I smiled to myself. Exposing Mick's attempt to keep the evidence to himself for his own benefit was a small victory. I didn't regret it one bit.

Mick walked over and handed the leather bag to the Police Chief, glaring at me as he went by. The Chief lifted the flap, unzipped the top, and pulled out a wallet, checking the identification inside. "Hmmm. This definitely belongs to our missing woman. She won't get far without her credit cards, license, and cash." He looked at me. "This makes me even more curious about what's happened to her. No woman I've ever known would last ten minutes without her credit cards."

Mick chuckled along with the Police Chief.

"Instead of insulting women, why don't you two do your job and find her," Tilly said, standing with her hands on her hips, scowling like she was ready to attack. "I mean, the trail's getting cold. What are you waiting for?" She even dared to clap her hands in a let's-get-going prompt.

"No need to get all in a huff, Tilly. We *are* following the trail." The Chief zipped the purse closed and limped toward the cruiser.

"We'll be back," Mick said to me as he followed behind Chief Bullock.

Tilly wiped her hands after they drove out like that inconvenience was taken care of. I wasn't so sure.

She marched toward the door. "I had to do something to get them out of here. Are we ready for the grand opening because customers will be here soon?"

"As ready as we'll ever be, even with this crazy morning. Where did Mick find Ginger's purse?" I asked, catching up to Tilly.

"On the ground under my car. He actually accused me of trying to hide evidence. Can you believe it?"

"Are you kidding me?" I said as we reached the front door of the shop. "It's me you're talking to, Tilly."

"Okay, I admit that I gave it a little tap with my foot. But all I was trying to do was slide it out of sight so we could look inside first," she said defensively. "I didn't even know it belonged to Ginger until Mick snooped inside."

"How did it get there, Tilly?" I stopped her from going inside and avoiding my questions. "What do you know about it?"

Tilly rolled her eyes like she was bored with this conversation. "The strap must have broken when she helped me out of my car. Remember? I tripped." She leaned close to me. "I hope that looked like a real accident. I planned that little distraction as soon as I saw that Ginger was a handful of trouble."

I had to smile. "It was good, Tilly, but I know that you're as sure-footed as a tightrope walker, so it didn't fool me." I picked up the basket with the kitten. "Look at what Chief Bullock found out back. I can't believe that someone left this poor kitty here."

Tilly's face collapsed into a mixture of smiles and concern. "Aww, so sweet." She stroked the kitten. "Once she's cleaned up, and the matted fur clumps are combed out of her long hair, she'll be gorgeous. She's at the right place to find a good home. I'm so proud of what you and Hitch are doing here," she said, giving me a rare compliment.

Then Tilly's eyes narrowed. "What's this?" she said. She pulled at the corner of something white stuck between the basket and the fleece blanket under the kitten, a piece of paper that had been folded several times into a small square.

I looked over Tilly's shoulder and read the note. "My name is Clawdia, please find me a good home."

"Clawdia?" I said. "How cute is that?"

I turned to take her inside just as Hitch came out and hung the *Open* flag next to the door and several cars pulled into the parking lot.

"The fun's about to begin," Tilly said, waving to the cars like she was our official 'meeter and greeter.'

Maybe the rest of the day would go smoothly.

Like I told myself earlier, I could hope.

6

Inside, I slipped the basket onto a stool and savored the last minute of quiet to look at the hard work we'd put in to get to this moment. The oak floor and counter glistened, the black iron tables and chairs were arranged in comfortable groups, and orchid blooms filled the windows with their unique beauty. Above our work area the chalkboard was filled with our selections from plain vanilla milkshakes to exotic mango ginger smoothies. Mouthwatering cupcakes, cookies, and donuts filled the pastry case, treats for the eyes and nose.

Hitch put his arm around my shoulders. "It came together perfectly, didn't it?"

"Yes, I think it did." I leaned my head in the

crook of his arm and inhaled the coffee aroma on his shirt. "Where's Conrad?"

Hitch pointed to the door at the other end of the shop. "He volunteered to hang out in the greenhouse with Jasper and the kittens. He pointed out that *someone* has to do that difficult job."

"I have something to show you," I said, and led him to the basket with the new kitten. "Look at this, Hitch. Chief Bullock found this basket out back when he was checking for clues about Ginger's disappearance." He peeked in and gave me a smile.

"Her name is Clawdia, with a W."

His head jerked up, then he laughed. "Clever. Poor thing, but with a good cleaning this little fur ball will be a stunner. I'll take this back for Conrad and Jasper to handle. You're okay here by yourself for a minute?" His concern for me and the kitten touched me deeply.

"Of course." As soon as Hitch disappeared with Clawdia, the door opened and Tilly ushered in three young boys, our first customers. They made a beeline for the glass case. Their dad followed behind. I'd seen him at the beach a few times always trying to keep up with his boys. Behind him, Tilly led a group of women inside.

I hustled behind the counter, pasted on a smile,

and said. "Who can I help first? We have all sorts of delicious shakes and smoothies to choose from."

"I want a donut," one of the boys yelled and pointed to a tray stacked with A Donut A Day specials.

"Me too."

"Me three."

That was easy once I got the nod from their dad. He smiled an easy smile. "And, two vanilla shakes and one chocolate shake for the kids. I'll try," he studied the chalkboard, "the chocolate swirl shake with whipped cream and walnuts. I'll need a long-handled spoon with that one, right?"

I chuckled at his concern. "You sure will unless you want to clog up your straw. I'll get right on these for you." I handed over the donuts and got busy with the rest of the order.

"What a great idea this is. I bet you'll be swamped," he said to me. "I know I'll be a regular with the boys. Is it okay if we go in the greenhouse while we wait? I probably shouldn't take them in though. I heard you have kittens looking for homes, and that's all the boys have been talking about. They're working on me constantly to adopt one."

"By all means. I'll find you out there when your shakes are ready. Just so you know, you'll have to fill in an application if you want to adopt and the kittens aren't ready to leave for another couple of weeks."

He sighed which made me think I'd just given him the excuse he needed to take this adoption step slowly.

Hitch returned, pushed me out of the way, and took over the shake orders. "You're better with the customers," he said, adding a wink.

"Tilly can bring the shakes out to the boys. Don't forget to add the long-handled spoons to get any chunks that don't fit in the straws," I told Hitch and turned to the next customer waiting to order. "Violet?" I almost choked at the sight of my frumpy, partly gray-haired neighbor. "What a... surprise." I tried to cover up my shock by quickly asking, "Did your friend ever show up?"

"Oh, yes," she said, waving away the issue as though it wasn't any concern. "She finally called when she arrived at the Bayside Bed and Breakfast where she's staying and said she'd join us here instead of stopping at my house."

Violet giggled, which sounded too girlie for this woman who looked at least ten years older than her forty-five years in her I-love-gardening t-shirt and elastic waist pants. "I shouldn't have panicked and called the police. But," Violet leaned over the counter and lowered her voice, "you can never be too careful, I always say. The world is full of dangerous people, you know."

I kept my face neutral thinking about all the times she'd called the police on Jasper, who was not a danger to anyone.

"Did you at least let the Police Chief know you've heard from Ginger? He was here looking for her, you know." I doubted that Violet would grasp my frustration of the morning police intrusion just before our opening, but it made *me* feel a little better to mention it.

"Of course, I did, Sunny. I know you think I'm nothing but a complaining busybody, but I have a very deep and caring streak. When Ginger said she'd be at my house by seven, of course I worried when she didn't show up. But it looks like everything is cleared up." Violet studied the chalkboard while she tapped on the counter. "I'll have a fresh cranberry and orange smoothie. That sounds refreshing and not too calorie-laden." She patted her hips and giggled again.

"Oh, Violet," I said, "Tell Ginger that the police have her pocketbook with her license, credit cards, and money. Apparently, she lost it in the parking lot this morning."

"Really? She didn't mention anything about that to me. I wonder how she checked in without her credit card." Violet shrugged like it wasn't her problem. "I'll be sure to let her know."

She turned around toward her companions. "Girls. Order whatever you want. It's my treat." She leaned forward and said in hushed tones, "These are my college roommates, Carla Singleton and Laura O'Brien. We're having a mini reunion weekend. That's why Ginger is here, too. It was her idea."

College roommates? That explained one mystery.

Laura, tall and walking like she had a broom handle up her spine, stepped to the counter. "I'll have the green smoothie, please." She wandered off with Violet after she'd ordered without offering any small talk.

Carla stepped up next, with enough personality for the entire trio. "What a cute place you have," she said. Her bubbly energy somehow matched her curly blonde hair that danced when she moved. She held her bangs out of her face with cute butterfly clips that added to her effervescence.

"Thanks. It's our grand opening today."

"You don't say. How lucky, right, Greg?" She turned to the tall, dark-haired handsome man next to her. "This is my husband. We met in college. One of those love at first sight moments that led to a happily ever after romance. Just like in a novel, right Greg?"

He nodded and said, "Yes, dear." He smiled at me, but his distracted look made me wonder if he shared Carla's romantic fairytale or had even heard her ramblings.

"I'll have a plain vanilla shake. Can you make it with low-fat yogurt?" she asked.

"Sure. And you, Greg?"

"Oh, nothing for me." His gaze wandered around the shop absent-mindedly. I guessed he'd rather be anywhere but here.

He pulled out his wallet to pay, but Carla playfully slapped his hand. "Violet's treating, dear. Now, put your wallet away." She wandered off to sit with Violet and Laura at one of the tables, leaving Greg standing awkwardly at the counter.

I wondered if Carla ordered him around like this all the time because his response was more robotic than animated.

"I changed my mind," he said. "I'll have that smoothie with coffee in it."

"The coffee, oat, and maple smoothie?"

"Yeah, sure. And, I'll pay for mine," he said

leaving no room for an argument, which I had no intention of giving him. He handed me a ten. "I think it was a big mistake coming here this weekend with these women. They're already driving me crazy."

"They seem like a nice bunch," I said, not sure how else to respond.

"That's because you don't know them. Since Violet is older than the other roommates, she likes to play mother to them."

I handed him his change, but he waved me off. "Keep it." He moseyed into the greenhouse while the three women sat and chatted.

"Here you go, ladies," I said delivering their shakes to their table. "It's a shame Ginger hasn't shown up yet."

Laura rolled her eyes. "It's just like Ginger to be all dramatic and then make her grand entrance. Violet let her know our plans so now it's up to her. This weekend was her idea to begin with, and I plan to have a good time. With or without Ginger." She dabbed a smear of green smoothie off her lip with a napkin.

Carla looked around in a bit of a panic. "Where'd Greg go? I should never have taken my eyes off him."

"Oh, honey," Laura covered Carla's hand with

her own. "Don't worry about him so much. Give him some space. And," she leaned closer to Carla, "stop with all the nagging."

Carla's spine stiffened "Nagging? I don't nag," she said with an unmistakable huffiness.

I sensed some trouble brewing between these old friends during this girl reunion weekend.

And where was Ginger?

7

The rest of opening day flew by in a blur. We blended shakes and served sweet tasty treats to the flood of customers that streamed into Shakes and Cakes.

Yes, a flood, which relieved my anxiety from the morning worries.

Every time Hitch walked by me, he whispered, "Ka-ching," and gave me two thumbs up.

The orchids, tropical plants, potted herbs and colorful hanging baskets racked up brisk sales, too. And, the best part was the long list of interested people signing up to adopt one of our fur balls looking for their forever home.

All in all, the day was a success but... isn't there always a but? I reminded myself. I couldn't shake

Ginger's early morning visit, disappearance, lost pocketbook, and the hints of trouble in the college roommates' weekend reunion.

Tilly served customers with friendly and appropriate conversation; Conrad chaperoned Jasper and the kittens, keeping sharp eyes on everyone going in and out of the greenhouse. By the end of our business day, the kittens were curled up in a kitty pile sleeping off all the excitement. Even Clawdia was back in her basket with her tail tucked around her nose.

"I'll meet you at your house?" Tilly said as she blended herself a concoction with who knew what was in it.

"Sounds good," I answered. The quiet after she left enveloped me like a soothing puff of warm scented air. I sank into one of the chairs at a round table, leaned back with my legs stretched out, and groaned. "It feels good to get off my feet, finally," I said to Hitch who pulled up a chair opposite me and sank down heavily.

"I think we hit it out of the park today." Beneath that enthusiasm, his eyes drooped with fatigue. "And I heard lots of customers say they plan to make this a regular stop in their day. And... the kittens. They are their own attraction." He jiggled my foot with his. "Right?"

I tried to ignore that contact but it sent goosebumps along my skin. "Yeah, lots of interest but I'm not surprised. There isn't anything much cuter than a soft kitty to cuddle... except a roly-poly puppy."

Hitch's eyes widened with what looked to be concern. "Is that next?"

I laughed at his shock. "No. At least I hope there isn't a need."

"Ready to go?" He stood up and held his hand out to me. His eyes had that special twinkle again that he'd lost after Ginger's unexpected visit. My heart did a little flip when I put my hand in his and he wrapped his strong fingers around mine. Friends, I reminded myself. We are only friends.

I heaved a big sigh and said, "After I double-check the kittens and convince Jasper that her job is done for the day, I'll be so ready for a hot bath and a glass of something to celebrate making it through our first day."

Hitch chuckled. "Jasper really takes that job seriously, doesn't she? I noticed that she got plenty of hugs and pats today, too. Good thing she's such a sweetheart."

"Unless someone crosses her. Her first priority is to keep those kittens safe. I'm sure of it."

We walked side by side into the greenhouse. Even with all the plant sales today, it barely made a dent in our tropical jungle atmosphere. Hitch had ordered that inventory well.

I gave a soft whistle. "Come on Jasper, time to head home." She perked up her ears and wagged her bushy tail before she lumbered around the Kitty Castle from kitten to kitten, bestowing a final sniff and a bit of slobber on each one. "She's making a final kitty count," I told Hitch before leading the way outside.

"What do you mean?"

I jostled him with my elbow. "Just kidding."

We strolled out into the late afternoon sunshine and my stomach dropped. The satisfied feeling from moments ago vanished like a burst soap bubble.

"What now?" I said as I watched a Pineville police cruiser pull in and stop only feet away from us.

Officer Walker unfolded himself from behind the wheel, stuck a toothpick in the corner of his mouth, and slammed his door closed. "Glad I caught both of you still here."

I had no idea why he just showed up, but my

instinct told me to head the conversation away from Hitch.

"Did Ginger Ross stop at the station to pick up her pocketbook?" I asked casually.

His brow furrowed. "Not yet. Why do you ask? Did she come back here looking for it?"

I noticed Walker giving Shakes and Cakes the once over. Did he think I was hiding Ms. Ross among the orchid plants or maybe the Kitty Castle?

I ignored his suspicious looks and said, "No, I haven't seen her since this morning, but I gave her friend, Violet Burnham, the message that you had her purse at the police station. I assumed she'd follow through. Violet did tell you that Ginger is staying at the Bayside Bed and Breakfast, right?"

Walker shifted his toothpick to the other side of his mouth. Some kind of acknowledgment that he heard me, I guess. "Yeah," he said, "I got that message from your neighbor... but there's a problem. The people at the bed and breakfast haven't seen hide nor hair of Ginger Ross except for her silver SUV in their lot. She never actually checked in and no one there saw Ms. Ross actually park her car. That's what brings me back here."

Walker paused and just stared at the two of us from behind his sunglasses. "From everything I've come up with, you were the last ones to see her." Mick let that last comment hang in the air as if he suspected we knew more than we'd told him. He leaned against his car, settling in for more than a quick visit. Not a good sign, but I wasn't going to let him rattle me.

"I don't know what to say, Mick," I said, exuding innocence as I shrugged my shoulders and looked to Hitch, perplexed and questioning. "Ginger was here when we arrived this morning. She showed up completely out of the blue, and she left when we said we were busy." I hoped this satisfied him but suspected it wouldn't.

"Out of the blue?" Mick held up a cell phone. "I found this in her car and one of our tech guys figured out her password. There are a bunch of calls to you, Mr. Hitchner. Care to explain?"

I felt Hitch's fingers squeeze my shoulder, but his voice remained calm. "There's nothing to explain," he said. "She did call me, but I didn't answer her calls... or the texts that you've probably found, too."

I didn't know where this might be going.

Walker kept chewing on his toothpick, like the cat that ate the canary. Did he know more than he was telling I wondered?

"But why all the attempts to contact you?" he

asked. "Violet said that Ginger was coming here this morning because she knew *you'd* be here. I find that to be a puzzling and interesting question. Especially now that she's missing."

I had to hand it to Hitch. His demeanor didn't change. He remained as cool and calm as the cucumbers in our breakfast smoothies. "You'll have to ask Ginger. I didn't talk to her and I don't know why she kept trying to contact me." He stared back at Mick. The two of them in a stand-off. One digging for information, the other poker-faced.

"That's what you told Chief Bullock this morning and unfortunately, we can't ask Ginger Ross *anything* if we can't find her." Mick was caving, his voice loud now and filled with frustration. "So, I'm asking you again, and you can cooperate here or come to the station: Why was Ginger Ross trying so hard to get in touch with you, Ty Hitchner?"

Walker eased forward an inch or two, putting himself in Hitch's face.

"I. Don't. Know," Hitch said through clenched teeth. "Ginger Ross does what she wants without input from me. I met her in New York when I was working there, but that's the extent of my dealings with her."

Walker's color was rising, and his eyes got wider

as he said, "That's not what Violet Burnham told me. She said that you and Ginger had a relationship." Mick's lip twitched when he glanced at me. I'm sure he hoped that comment would upset me, but I knew how Mick liked to play games with people. He relished having the power to stick in a verbal knife and twist it.

"I wonder," Hitch said, "if I told you that Violet Burnham is in a relationship with the Police Chief, would you believe that, too? There was no romance between Ginger and me regardless of what rumor you've heard. No romance and no relationship."

I tried as hard as I could to keep my anger from boiling over. "Mick," I said, "Violet told us that Ginger planned a weekend reunion with her college roommates. The four women—Violet, Ginger, Laura O'Brien, and Carla Singleton—are all here in town along with Carla's husband, Greg. Have you asked *them* any questions?"

To my surprise, Mick pulled out a small notebook and scribbled something down. "Do you know where those women are staying? How I can find them?"

"Not a clue. Ask Violet." What the heck had he been doing all day? I wondered.

Officer Walker nodded, tucked his notebook in his pocket, got back in his car, and drove off.

"That was weird." I said. "What do you think is going on with Ginger? I don't know about you, Hitch, but I've got a really bad feeling about this situation."

Jasper pulled on her leash and headed for the Camaro. Was she done with opening day festivities? We followed behind and Hitch opened the door for us. As Jasper leaped into the back seat, he said, "Listen, Sunny, I know all this is upsetting but what Ginger does is completely out of our control. Let's think about *us*. Okay? How does this sound? I'll drop you and Jasper off at home, pick up a bottle of champagne that's chilling in my fridge, and come back for a little celebration. We've earned it."

I climbed into my seat and smiled up at him, thinking his plan sounded *almost* perfect. He walked around to his door and got in. "I've got a better idea," I said. He quickly glanced in my direction while he drove out of the parking lot, a worried expression etched on his tired face. "Just go straight to your apartment. No need to drop me off first, that's just a waste of time."

He let out a deep belly laugh. "That's a much

better plan, Sunshine. Thanks." His face broke into a wide grin and he patted my thigh.

"Thanks for what?"

"For being so smart and coming up with great ideas."

Okay, I knew he was exaggerating but it still made me feel like a million bucks.

He pulled into the driveway of his apartment. "Want to come in or wait here? It'll only take a minute to grab the champagne."

"Put the windows down for Jasper and I'll come in. She's completely pooped, anyway, after her long day as Chief Kitty Nanny." I reached over the seat and ruffled her ear. "Right?" She groaned but didn't even open her eyes.

I followed Hitch up the porch steps to his apartment in a two-family house. I hadn't seen the inside since he'd come back from New York. I guess you could say I was feeling curious about his bachelor pad.

"After you, Madam," he said with an exaggerated and very bad stilted accent as he held his hand out for me to go inside first. "Ignore the mess, I wasn't expecting company," he added.

"What mess?" I said as I scanned his tidy living room.

He laughed. "See, it worked. You thought the place would be trashed so now you won't even notice a few dust bunnies. I left the champagne in the kitchen. Be right back." He walked away chuckling about his clever reverse psychology.

I slowly moved around the room. His comfortable furniture made for cozy seating, but what caught my attention were the orchid photographs hanging on his white walls. "Did you take these photographs, Hitch?" I called out to him.

I heard footsteps behind me and turned around to ask my question again, assuming he hadn't heard me the first time. "Did—"

One look at his face gave me concern. His normal tan coloring had drained to a pasty white hue. "What's wrong? Did someone steal your champagne?" I joked.

"Ginger's in the kitchen."

"What?" Now, it was my turn to panic. "She's been hiding here?"

He shook his head. I couldn't remember ever seeing Hitch at a loss for words.

"I think she broke in."

"Well, tell her to leave." I started to walk toward his kitchen. "I'll tell her myself if you won't."

Hitch grabbed my arm, stopped me, and pulled

me close. His hand trembled. "Don't go in there, Sunny."

"Why not, Hitch?" He was really scaring me with his tight grip.

"Ginger's dead. She's lying on the kitchen floor. Dead. I'm no expert but I think she may have been poisoned."

8

I sank onto the nearest chair, my legs turned to jelly, "Dead? Poisoned?"

"I didn't spend much time examining her, but I didn't see any blood or obvious injury. It looked like she threw up a blueish mess that matched a spilled drink on the counter."

I guess I must have looked confused and startled. This was all too much to process. "How do you even know this, Hitch?"

"During my security guard training," he said. "I participated in a specialized workshop on unusual murder techniques used by killers. We learned how to diagnose symptoms, recognize odors, and were told how to respond in different situations. Unfortunately for Ginger, we arrived too late to help her."

I couldn't get my head wrapped around how this was even possible. How had Hitch's work in New York caused him so much trouble? First, when his previous boss was murdered, and now this woman following him here with her problems?

He stood in front of his window, like that would provide answers to this crazy situation. Then, he took out his phone. "I'm calling 9-1-1."

I tuned out his conversation as my mind replayed the day's events. At least, I told myself, there was no way that Hitch could be accused of murdering Ginger Ross. He'd been with me all day right up until he found her body. There were plenty of customers to vouch for his whereabouts if Officer Walker decided I'd say anything to protect Hitch.

Too many questions swirled in my brain. How did Ginger get inside Hitch's house? Who followed her and why? Where was the killer now?

"She must have walked here," Hitch said, reading my thoughts like he was so good at doing. He paced back and forth across the room, head down, and hands in his pockets. "Maybe there really was someone stalking her," he muttered then stopped and looked at me. "One of those roommates in town for the reunion?"

"That makes some sense because who else could have known she was here in Pineville?" I said.

Someone knocked on the front door. "Hitch? Are you inside?"

"What's Tilly doing here?" he said as he opened the door.

She entered without waiting for an invitation. "Did you two decide to ditch me and have a little celebration on your own?"

"Not exactly," I said.

"What's going on?" She looked from me then to Hitch. "You both look like this was the worst day of your lives instead of a smashing success at your grand opening. I mean, come on—what's with the gloomy faces?"

"Hitch found Ginger in the kitchen," seemed to be the easiest answer.

"Well, isn't that a coincidence. I saw her walking in this direction after I left Shakes and Cakes. She was hustling right along not far from the Bayside Bed and Breakfast like she was late for an important meeting. It didn't make sense why she was walking instead of driving that giant SUV. I even thought about stopping to give her a ride but," Tilly chuckled, "that idea only lasted for a second and a half."

"Did you talk to her?" The last thing that I

wanted to hear was that Tilly had any kind of interaction with a woman who was now dead. Especially after her dealings with Officer Walker about Ginger's pocketbook.

"Are you kidding me? I zipped right by and waved." Tilly demonstrated a little finger wiggle. "I don't think she even noticed."

That was a relief.

"And then I stopped here to pick up my hammer that Hitch borrowed." She looked around the room. "Nice job hanging up your photos, by the way. It looks like a gallery in here. Anyway, I was so distracted hunting for my hammer that I couldn't find by the way, that I think I left my smoothie in your kitchen. I'll go check."

I'd never been good at keeping a poker face. She stopped and stared at me. "What? Hitch doesn't care if I come in his apartment. He wouldn't have told me where he keeps the key if he minded. Right, Hitch?"

"That's right, Tilly, but there's something you don't understand," he said.

Sirens screamed on the street, stopping outside Hitch's house.

I put my hand on Tilly's arm to keep her from investigating any further. She looked at my hand, and her brow furrowed with confusion.

"When I said Ginger's in the kitchen, I should have added, she's dead. Hitch thinks she was poisoned," I added, just before Hitch opened the door for Police Chief Bullock and Officer Walker. I didn't want Tilly to be blind-sided by that detail and blurt out something to incriminate herself, like everything she'd just told us.

Tilly sank onto a chair. The knowledge that she'd been here, at the scene of a murder, and left possible evidence that could be incriminating must have hit as hard as if Jasper crashed into her from behind.

She looked at me with wide eyes, and I zipped my fingers across my mouth hoping she got my message. She bit her lip, so I guess she did.

"You found Ginger Ross?" Police Chief Bullock asked after he walked inside.

"What's she doing here?" Officer Walker sneered. "I was with you and Sunny only a short time ago, and you said you didn't know her whereabouts. Are you trying to tell us she just showed up *at your house* out of the blue?"

Before Hitch had a chance to answer, I said, "That's exactly what happened and I'm glad you remember seeing us at Shakes and Cakes." My voice sounded testy even to my ears.

"Okay, calm down. Where is she?" Chief Bullock asked, his face drawn. "A lot of people are concerned about her, so let's get this mystery wrapped up. It's been a long day, and I, for one, am ready to head home."

That wasn't going to happen.

"In the kitchen," Hitch said. "She's dead."

That comment sucked all the air out of the house as the two policemen dropped their jaws and stared at him.

"She's dead. Here in your house. How did *that* happen?" the Chief asked. I couldn't miss his suspicion-laced undertone.

Hitch shook his head. "I have no idea. Sunny and I stopped here on the way to her house, and I found Ginger in the kitchen. I haven't touched or moved anything."

The Chief spun around. "And Tilly? What are you doing here?"

"Just visiting with my friends," she said and added a smile that looked forced from my perspective.

"Wait here," the Police Chief said. He motioned to Mick, and they disappeared into Hitch's kitchen.

"What do we do now?" I whispered to Hitch. "Jasper's in the car, I really want to take a shower and get some clean clothes on." I couldn't help myself, I shuddered, forcing back a sob. "It's just creepy knowing there's a body in your kitchen."

I know I sounded whiny but, yeah, I was tired and feeling a little claustrophobic. And scared. And honestly? Sorry for myself.

Before Hitch had time to calm me down, Chief Bullock returned to the living room. "We're going to seal this whole apartment and treat this as a suspicious death. Go to Sunny's house and wait there. That way, I'll know where to find you when we have more questions."

That sounded perfect to me. Or as perfect as anything this messed up could be.

"Oh," The Chief held his finger up. "Hitch, there's a Shakes and Cakes cup spilled on the counter. Is it yours?"

"No. I suppose Ginger brought it and set it down there," Hitch said without skipping a beat.

I hoped that lie didn't come back to haunt any of us one day.

9

Without waiting for Police Chief Bullock to change his mind or ask more questions, we scooted out of Hitch's apartment and drove to my house. It wouldn't be easy to keep my mind off the crime scene and what it might mean for Hitch, but at least I'd be in my own house with Jasper, the two kittens, Hitch, and Tilly. We'd be able to wait and wonder what had happened to Ginger Ross together.

Once inside, Tilly, without a trace of her earlier fear, announced, "We need to make a list of every possible suspect before the police discover my fingerprints on that Shakes and Cakes cup."

She had a point but one we could work around.

"Of course, your prints are on the cup, Tilly, you served it. And that's the story we're sticking to."

"Perfect." She retrieved a bottle of champagne from her tote bag and handed it to me, "I bought this for you two to celebrate. Let's have a toast to today's success."

"Great minds think alike, right, Sunny?" Hitch said with a grin across his face. "I'm referring to Tilly and me, in case you were wondering."

I waved them both out to the back yard where I had a comfortable patio surrounded by my flower garden. "I'll bring out glasses and whatever else I can find to go with champagne."

"Strawberries? Isn't that a thing?" Tilly asked holding the door open.

"It might be, but it's not on my menu tonight. You'll be lucky if I can round up crackers and cheese. Now, shoo." I waved them out with both hands.

"First things first, right Jasper?" I said when they were gone. She'd been sitting patiently in front of her bowl. I poured a serving of her dry food and added a bit of water, just how she liked it.

"And, you, too," I said to Princess Muffin and Stash. They mewed and looked up at me like they'd been neglected for weeks. With dinner chores done, I put three champagne flutes on a tray, found an unopened box of crackers in my cupboard, and inspected my package of cheddar cheese in my fridge. "Not moldy yet," I declared to the animals. "It will do." I carried it all outside.

The door slammed behind me. Tilly turned around in her patio chair with her finger to her lips shushing me as she nodded toward my neighbor's yard next door.

"What?" I mouthed almost silently.

"Violet and her friends are talking about Ginger," she whispered.

My ears pricked up. I set the tray down, hoping we'd hear some tidbit of important information.

"Shouldn't we tell them she's dead?" I whispered.

"Not yet," Tilly hissed back at me. She tiptoed to the fence that separated my yard from Violet's. Not that my neighbors could hear her silent footsteps on the grass, but Tilly loved to be overly dramatic.

Hitch opened the champagne with a loud *pop*, earning a dirty look from Tilly who stood between two shrubs with her ear against my cedar privacy fence. He filled two glasses, leaving the third empty. I guess he decided that Tilly was too busy eavesdropping, so why waste any on her. Then, he bent down and picked a few cosmos from my flower bed, handing them to me along with a glass of champagne.

I was touched by his gesture and this welcome distraction from Tilly's outlandish behavior.

He held his glass up and whispered, "To us, Sunny Shaw, and to more success at Shakes and Cakes." We clinked our glasses together.

This simple act, and Hitch's dazzling smile, gave me a giddy feeling even before I tasted the bubbly.

Tilly returned just as we took that first sip. "I'm going next door," she announced as she marched along the path to the front of my house.

Hitch gave me a little tap. "You'd better go with her, Sunny. Who knows what kind of trouble she'll start? I'll wait here so it doesn't look like a grand invasion."

"Sure, Hitch. You just want to enjoy the champagne," I teased. "Don't drink it all. And keep Jasper here. Violet will call the cops if she even thinks Jasper might trample one of her posies."

I quickly chugged half my glass of bubbly, hoping it would relax my tingling nerves before I dashed after Tilly. I caught up with her just as she reached the sidewalk.

"What's your plan?" I asked, slightly out of breath.

"Who needs a plan? I like to wing it."

Great. I had a sinking feeling about this expedition, but it was too late to back out and finish the champagne with Hitch. A much more enjoyable option.

Tilly marched right past Violet's perennial flower bed filled with blues, yellows, and a splash of red blooms. She continued around the side of her house and proceeded straight to Violet's backyard. We were practically on top of the three women before Violet startled at the sight of her intruders. She looked at us and shaded her eyes. "What are *you* two doing here?"

"Hello to you, too, Violet," Tilly said in a sugary sweet tone. Without an invitation, which I knew wouldn't come, she pulled over an empty chair and sat down next to Violet. Making a point of leaning away from Tilly, Violet set her wine glass down, sloshing some over the edge.

"What do you think you're doing, Tilly?" Violet waved one hand around the circle of women. "As I suppose you can see, I have guests, and I don't remember inviting *you* to pop over."

I had to cover a laugh with a fake cough. Tilly had never just *popped over* to visit Violet.

"Oh. Sorry." Tilly looked around the group,

smiling an oversized apology but making no move to leave. I waited in the background to see what would happen next.

Carla, bubbling with energy, perched at the edge of her chair. She removed her floppy straw hat and fluffed her blonde curls like she was getting ready for a bit of entertainment. Laura, the third member of this trio, sat tall and still. She was the observer in the group, holding her cards close as she waited for events to unfold.

"Weren't there supposed to be four of you?" Tilly asked with her brow in a quizzical line like this was just way too much for her to comprehend. "And what about that handsome man that came into Shakes and Cakes this morning with you all? What was his name?" She rolled her eyes to the sky as if it held the answer.

Carla lifted her hand like she was in a classroom. "That would be Greg, my husband. He volunteered to pick up chowder and lobster rolls from the Little Dog Diner in Misty Harbor. Violet said they have the *best* seafood around." She took a quick look at her watch and scowled. "He should have been back by now," and quickly covered with a, "maybe it was busy."

With the way she nagged him when they were at

Shakes and Cakes, I supposed she also kept an eagle eye on his comings and goings. If he didn't have a good excuse for being late, I suspected he'd get a tongue lashing.

Tilly picked up the bottle of wine like she was the hostess and topped off all the glasses. "Just have more wine while you wait. I'm sure Greg just got sidetracked at the diner talking to the locals about all the attractions."

Carla's mouth dropped open, but Tilly was too quick for her.

"I mean, does he really want to sit here with you three gossipy women?"

I decided Tilly was here for the long haul, so I sat down next to Laura. She hadn't said a word, smiled, or even sipped her wine. While Carla and Violet were more or less open books, I couldn't figure out what Laura was thinking.

"So, Laura, do all of you get together often?" I asked, thinking it was the best place to start the conversation.

It took her a couple of seconds to realize I was talking to her, but she finally turned toward me. "It's been awhile since all four of us planned a weekend together. But this was Ginger's idea, and," she rolled her eyes, "what Ginger wants, Ginger gets."

"Interesting," I said. "Where *is* Ginger?"

That question hung in the air as all eyes turned to me.

Violet took a sip of her wine. "I wish I knew," she said when she had an audience. "She's being very rude to keep us wondering about what she's up to."

"That's right," Carla piped in. "Don't get me wrong because Ginger can be very generous but... I'm not sure how I should put this. She can also get a bug up her butt over nothing."

She put her straw hat back on and pulled it down over her forehead as if it could hide her real feelings about Ginger which, by the expression on her face, I took to be quite low.

Laura pushed a few stray hairs away from her face and said quietly, "I've been wondering if Ginger invited us all to meet her but never even intended to show up."

"That doesn't make sense," Violet sputtered. "She sounded excited when she called me about seeing everyone."

By now, it seemed as if the three women had forgotten that Tilly and I were part of the group. They threw their comments back and forth, not worried about hiding any secrets.

"Why would she do that?" Carla demanded. She

leaned forward like she was about to attack Laura. "You sound just like when we were in college and you always thought you knew better than the rest of us." She checked her watch again and mumbled, "Where the heck is Greg? I have a mind to just go home when he finally shows up."

"I wonder," Tilly said, with a mischievous gleam in her eyes, "if Greg and Ginger met up and decided to go off for some sightseeing together."

Did I hear right? What was Tilly up to?

Laura smirked. Violet's eyes popped open wide. The color of Carla's face flared like an overripe tomato.

Oh boy, this group wasn't as kissy and cozy as I thought.

Did one of them dislike Ginger enough to kill her?

10

Tilly's outrageous suggestion linking Ginger and Greg no doubt had everyone imagining them on an outing together, judging from the shocked silence that hung in the air. Finally, a car door slammed outside Violet's house.

Carla jumped to her feet, threw her hat on the chair, and fluffed her curls back into place. "That must be Greg," she said, Relief flooded her face and her voice, giddy with delight, rose an octave. Instead of taking the path, she jumped over Violet's flower bed and ran to the front of the house.

Tilly leaned over to Violet. "Is her marriage in trouble?" she stage whispered so everyone could hear. "She acts so desperate. I mean, she doesn't even give the guy a little bit of rope. I'd guess she doesn't trust him for a second."

Violet's mouth dropped open, but no words came out. I still couldn't figure out the game Tilly was playing.

Laura laughed, the first show of emotion I'd seen yet. "Greg's a big flirt," she said. "You'll see when he gets here. I think he does it to annoy Carla. But, marriage trouble? No idea. I have no experience on *that* subject."

With her brusque personality? No surprise there.

I waited expectantly, almost believing the couple would arrive hand in hand and hoping that Tilly would finally decide this was the time for us to exit. But, from what I could tell, she was settling in and not making any move to depart.

Voices drifted ahead of the people walking toward us.

"I hear Carla, but that other voice doesn't sound like Greg," Violet said. She looked at Tilly and frowned. "This is all your fault."

"Me? What on earth are you talking about?"

And then, Carla, escorted by Police Chief Bullock and Officer Walker, appeared around the corner.

"Ladies," the Police Chief said, nodding to each of us.

Violet jumped out of her chair. "What's going on?" Did something happen to Ginger?"

"Or, Greg?" Laura added, showing a spark of emotion.

"I have a few questions, so please be seated." Chief Bullock patted the air in a calming gesture. He looked at Tilly and me with one eyebrow ticked up but didn't say anything about our presence. Yet.

Violet plopped back onto her chair, looking none too happy about the Chief's command.

"Just a friendly hello to Sunny's neighbors," Tilly offered, without being asked, as she stood up. "We'll be right next door at Sunny's house in case you need us."

I noticed a bit of nervous trembling in her voice. Having the party crashed by the police was not part of her neighborly visit when we'd interrupted Violet's get-together.

"Sit down Tilly. I need to talk to you and Sunny, too."

Officer Walker stood just behind the Chief with his arms crossed and the toothpick in the corner of his mouth bobbing ferociously. If he wasn't careful, he'd end up with splinters in his tongue.

The image made me smirk a little until he glared my way.

The Chief took out a notebook and pencil. "Okay. Violet, how about you tell me who's who here."

She cleared her throat as if she were about to give a speech. Then she went around the group clockwise. "That's Carla Singleton with the curly hair and that's Laura O'Brien next to her. We were roommates in college along with Ginger Ross. The four of us were as thick as thieves as the saying goes," she rattled on in a nervous chatter. "We—"

The Chief interrupted. "Pleased to meet you ladies," he said and nodded politely. "Now, about your friend Ginger. Violet? You called in a missing person alert this morning. Tell me what you know about Ginger's plans."

"Like I already told you," she said sounding put out by having to repeat herself. "She promised to stop here at my house this morning by seven. You don't know Ginger but, believe me, she's the kind of person who is *never* late." She looked around the group for corroboration. "Right girls? I mean Carla sashays in at least a half hour late, and Laura is *usually* on time. But Ginger? Never, never late."

That was Violet, mistress of tact.

"Until today," Laura mumbled.

Carla only nodded, and I wasn't even sure she was paying attention because she kept looking toward the road.

"And that's why I called you, Chief Bullock," Violet said and clasped her hands together on her lap.

"And what were your plans today?" the Chief asked.

"Well," Violet said with a self-satisfied smirk, obviously reveling in her leadership role, "our first stop was at the Shakes and Cakes grand opening and we," she made a circle with her finger to include Carla and Laura, "plus Carla's husband, thought that maybe Ginger would find us there. But she never showed up."

"And, was Ginger planning to stay here with you, Violet?" the Chief asked.

"Oh, my goodness no." She shook her head for extra emphasis. "My house isn't grand enough for Ginger. She made reservations at the Bayside Bed and Breakfast in town for herself, Laura, and Carla. She was treating, right girls?" Violet seemed to love adding in that detail. Maybe it made her feel superior to have a wealthy friend.

A car door slammed out front. Carla shot up like

she'd been ejected from her chair. She charged toward the road before the Chief or Officer Walker had a chance to object.

"Greg! Where have you been?" I cringed at Carla's screech that ricocheted straight down Cobbler Lane for everyone to hear.

"Who's that?" the Chief asked, swiveling his head to watch Carla disappear.

"That's Greg, Carla's husband. He volunteered to drive to Misty Harbor to pick up our dinner. I suppose, *now*, we'll be eating cold chowder and soggy lobster rolls."

Violet picked at something on her pants, probably afraid to look at the Chief after her display of juvenile whining.

The Chief, to his credit, ignored Violet's dig and jotted down more notes. As I watched the events unfold, I wondered how exactly Greg had spent his time. From Carla's reaction, he took much too long to make this dinner run. And considering Laura's comment about his flirtatious streak, my goodness. That added an interesting layer of drama to the whole picture.

Carla reappeared holding onto Greg's arm like a vice and dragging him into the back yard. All eyes turned to the odd couple. "Come *on*, Greg," Carla said in a sugary voice. "The police have information about Ginger."

Greg's eyes flicked toward Chief Bullock. He clenched his jaw and wrinkled his brow. "What do you mean, Carla?" he said. "I saw Ginger walking along the road when I drove to Misty Harbor. I pulled over to ask if she needed a ride, but she said she was all set."

"You didn't ask her what she'd been doing all day and why she didn't join us?" Violet asked, obviously miffed.

Greg shrugged his shoulders and looked at Carla before answering, as if needing permission. "She didn't give me a chance. She walked away, up a driveway toward what looked to be a two-family house."

"How about you two have a seat over here," Chief Bullock said as he pointed to an empty chair next to Carla's seat.

My stomach twisted in a knot. The anticipation was killing me.

I risked a glance at Tilly. Her eyes were focused on Violet who sat with her lips clamped in a thin line. Laura had what looked like a smirk on her face. Carla scooched closer to Greg, grabbed his hand and squeezed until her knuckles turned white. Greg stared at the ground between his feet.

How would these long-time friends react when the Chief dropped his bombshell about Ginger's death?

And, more importantly, which one of them already knew exactly what had happened?

11

"I have some bad news," Chief Bullock said. He walked closer to where Violet perched at the head of the group. His limp more pronounced now, since he'd been standing for a stretch of time.

"What... what do you mean?" Violet's voice trembled as she looked at the Chief and then at Laura and Carla.

Carla pulled Greg's hand to her chest and covered her mouth with her other hand.

Laura shifted in her chair and fiddled with the top button of her blouse.

Greg dropped his head into his free hand.

Tilly's eyes widened like she was excited and

more than ready to hear how this was about to unfold.

"What Chief Bullock is trying to say," Officer Walker strode next to the Chief, "is that your friend, Ginger, is dead."

No soft announcement with a touch of compassion, just boom, to the point.

If looks could kill, the Chief's deep scowl would have flattened Officer Walker with his glare. I sensed there was no love lost between those two but that wasn't my problem. I did, however, think Mick's blunt statement was intended for its shock value to get everyone's' reaction.

It worked.

Greg's head shot up and he gave Walker a wild-eyed look.

Violet let out a delayed high-pitched screech and jumped out of her chair, sending it tipping backwards with a crash on the stone patio.

"What do you mean? I talked to Ginger this morning. Greg just said he saw her walking when he drove to Misty Harbor. Ginger organized this whole weekend. She can't be dead. Right, girls?"

She looked at Carla and Laura for confirmation even though her voice held a cupful of doubt.

"Yes, ladies," the Chief said. "Officer Walker is correct. I'm very sorry for your loss, and that's what makes this visit so much more painful. I need to ask each of you some questions. Let's see," he consulted his notes. "Violet, how about you come with me first. Is there a room inside where we can talk?"

"Inside? What's wrong with out here?" She clamped her fists on her hips as if she thought she actually had any control over the proceedings. "I have nothing to hide from my friends."

"I'm sure you don't," the Chief held his arm out. "Inside, Violet. Officer Walker will stay out here until I'm ready for the next person."

Mick's toothpick got busy again in the corner of his mouth. I assumed it meant he wasn't happy to be left out of the questioning, but the Chief needed someone to keep watch over the rest of us so we didn't take off.

The Chief stopped when he reached the back door of Violet's house. "Tilly and Sunny, you can wait at your house. Don't leave. I'll find you there."

That sounded fine with me. Maybe he didn't want us blabbering about what we knew about the crime scene. He must have concluded that we hadn't already told the others about Ginger's fate since they did look genuinely shocked. Grilling Greg about his whereabouts would have to wait.

"Come on, Tilly," I said as I stood up. "You heard the Chief."

Carla, Laura, and Greg sat in stunned silence as we walked past them. Mick smirked when my eyes met his. "Don't get any ideas, you two," he said.

"Like what?"

"Like warning Hitchner to make himself scarce. I saw his car at your house, and if he knows what's good for him, he'd better still be there when we come over. He has a lot of explaining to do." And with that statement, Mick's face spread in what I could only describe as an evil sneer.

I'd never felt so much anger toward this man as I did at that moment. The thought of Mick having a crush on me made my skin crawl and that shower I'd been looking forward to felt more urgent than ever. First, to clean off the day's grime from the satisfying hard work but more importantly, to scald off the layer of grunge that covered me from Mick's leer. Is that why he was coming down so hard on Hitch? His raging jealousy over our friendship? Even if Hitch wasn't in the picture, I wouldn't give that creepy guy the time of day.

Tilly pulled me away from the group. I snapped my mouth closed before I let something fall out that I'd surely regret and stomped along doing my best to calm down until we were at a safe distance away. Then, I let loose.

"What was his comment about Hitch supposed to mean?" I shook with fury.

Tilly kept her grip on my arm and kept me moving. "Let it go, Sunny. Mick wants to get under your skin. Don't let him or he wins this battle. We have to keep our cool and stay ten steps ahead of him."

She laughed, loosened her grip, and wrapped her arm around my shoulders. "That shouldn't be too hard. We've got this... you, me, and Hitch. And, don't forget it."

She was right. I thanked my lucky stars that Tilly was on my side with her shrewd mind and clever ideas.

Jasper must have heard us talking because she raced from the backyard and practically tackled me to the ground. But I was ready this time. "Oh, no you don't." I braced myself, lowering my center of gravity and welcomed her enthusiastic lunge without a mishap.

"Finally," Hitch said, appearing not far behind Jasper, worry etched on his face. "What the heck was going on in Violet's backyard for the last hour? I couldn't hear much through the fence since I was busy distracting Jasper from charging over to find you. And, to be honest, I thought about letting her go so I had an excuse to follow her to Violet's yard."

"It's probably best you didn't show up. Mick's on the prowl. I got the feeling he'd like to nail you with something connected to all this," Tilly said.

"He just has it in for you, and he'd nail you for letting the grass grow too long if he could," I said.

Hitch put his arm around me and pulled me toward the door. I was drained. "Let's go inside," I said. "We probably don't have much time before Chief Bullock and Mick come over to question us."

I opened my front door and followed Tilly, Hitch, and Jasper into the relative quiet and safety of my living room.

Stash fluffed her tail as big as a bottle brush, and Princess Muffin gave a pathetic hiss. They both arched their backs from their resting spot on the couch. They didn't fool anyone, least of all, Jasper. She wagged her tail and sniffed each kitty and let each one bat her nose without flinching. I laughed at their antics. "Sorry that we disturbed your naps, kitties." I gave a silent thanks for small wonders that packed such a huge dose of pleasure.

"I'll be right back with the rest of the champagne," Hitch said. "I left it in the kitchen, and I see no reason to let it go to waste."

"I won't argue with *that* plan," I said, "but we'd better keep our wits about us."

"Oh, pshaw," Tilly flapped her hand at me. "One glass of bubbly will take the edge off and make us that much sharper when the Chief and Mick show up. We can't overdo it with only one bottle for the three of us. Now, what have you got in your fridge to go with the champagne? I'm hungry."

Of course, she was. Drama was to Tilly as food was to me. I followed Hitch into the kitchen, and he surprised me with a bear hug. I let myself relax in his strong arms. "You look like you've been through the wringer," he said and rested his chin on my head.

"I'm really worried, Hitch. Mick has it in for you, and with Ginger found dead in your apartment, he'll try his hardest to make it look like you killed her."

"That's ridiculous. I was with you at Shakes and Cakes all day. Stop worrying."

I couldn't.

There were too many clues pointing straight at Hitch.

We had to figure out what happened before Mick found a way to turn the evidence against him. I didn't doubt that he'd do it if he could.

12

As Hitch, Tilly, and I sat around my kitchen table, enjoying champagne and grilled cheese sandwiches, I wondered if anyone had ever paired those two items together before. The bubbles and melted cheese between crisp bread worked great in my opinion. Tilly even reached over and stole an extra half from Hitch's plate.

"What?" she asked as I attempted to slap her hand. "I worked up an appetite over at Violet's house. Getting those women talking was hard work."

"I doubt it was for you, Tilly." Hitch washed down the last bite of his grilled cheese with the rest of his champagne, leaned back, and sighed with satisfaction. "I'm not sure anything ever tasted so delicious. Thanks, Sunny."

Tilly stacked the empty plates and dumped them in the sink with a clatter before she opened my freezer. "Well, looky here. Mint chocolate chip ice cream. I think after the day we've had, we all deserve to share it right out of the carton."

She slid two spoons on the table, keeping the third one for herself and dug out a big scoop. "Ooh, brain freeze." Her whole face puckered like an old dried apple.

I got three bowls, wrenched the ice cream from Tilly and dished out helpings for each of us. "You can eat out of the container at your house, but here we'll be more civilized."

The sound of spoons tapping on bowls was a welcome respite from conversation, even if it only lasted for a few minutes. After everything that had overloaded my senses today, I relished the food and quiet.

"Sunny," Tilly said after she'd scraped her bowl clean. "Can I have more?" She tilted her head like a little girl with big wishful eyes.

I laughed at her act. "Help yourself," I said, and slid the ice cream across the table.

As she scooped out more, she asked. "What's your take on Greg telling everyone that he saw Ginger walking when he drove to Misty Harbor?"

"What?" Hitch leaned forward. "That puts him near her when she was practically at my house. Maybe he did more than just see her. Where was she when *you* saw her, Tilly?"

She tapped her fingers on the table while she savored her last mouthful of ice cream, then smacked her lips. "She wasn't far from the Bayside Bed and Breakfast, so still about a mile from your house, Hitch. At least a twenty-minute walk. That means I had time to stop at your house, look for my hammer, and leave before Ginger arrived and Greg saw her."

"Could he be her stalker?" I asked, licking my spoon for the last dregs of ice cream.

"That's something to consider since it puts him at the scene of the crime, but what's his motive? And, how did he kill her, if he did?" Hitch stood up and put the ice cream back in the freezer.

We were grasping at straws, but this angle was the best we had to keep the focus off Hitch. The fact that Ginger was murdered in his kitchen left so many questions unanswered.

A knock at the door and Jasper let out one of her house-rattling barks. I jumped, sending Stash off my lap and straight to her hiding spot under the couch.

"The Chief, probably," I said. "I can't imagine what questions they'll have for us."

I opened the front door and tried to hold Jasper at bay with my leg. "Come in, I guess." I said to the Chief and Mick. It felt like I was preparing myself for a dose of disgusting medicine or even a walk off a gangplank into shark-infested waters.

Jasper sniffed the two men then returned to her favorite spot in the middle of the rug.

Mick scanned my living room. "Are you alone?" he asked, obviously annoyed.

"Umm... no. Jasper, Stash and Princess Muffin are here with me." I knew that's not what he meant, but I wasn't about to make this easy for them.

"Cut the cutesy-pie answers, Sunny. Where are Tilly and Hitchner?"

"Oh." I swept my arm around my living room. "So sorry. I thought you meant here in this room. Tilly and Hitch are in the kitchen."

Mick stormed past me, anger spilling off him like a bad case of dandruff. "Champagne?" I heard him say with disgust. "An interesting choice of drinks after a body was discovered in your kitchen, Hitchner. And the victim was a person you admitted you'd been avoiding."

I didn't hear Hitch reply, which was smart on his

part. I could just see his jaw clamped tight since he knew better than to engage with Mick's comments.

Tilly, on the other hand, used the situation to her advantage. "Mick, do you have anything productive to say or do you just like to hear the sound of your own voice? Because you've got a murder to solve and harassing us is not advancing that agenda."

I looked at the Chief. When was he planning to take control of this situation?

"Sunny," he said, ignoring Mick's outburst. "I have to ask you some questions."

I tried my best to focus on the Chief and at the same time listen to Tilly, but it wasn't working. I'd have to just have some faith that she'd manage Mick and verbally back him into a corner. He wouldn't like it but putting him on the defensive was the best option at the moment. If anyone could do that, it was Tilly.

Chief Bullock leaned on the back of one of my chairs. He didn't even try to hide the pain in his hip. "Mind if I sit down, Sunny?"

"Please do." I gestured to the chair and I sat opposite him on my couch. The two kittens peeked out from between my feet. Without pausing, Princess Muffin jumped on the Chief's lap while Stash joined me. What had felt like an interrogation moments ago, now morphed into what seemed more like two friends talking.

The Chief wasn't really a bad guy. His tenure as the Pineville Police Chief had racked up respect throughout our town, unlike Mick Walker.

He stroked the Princess and let out a sigh. "I need to put a timeline together, Sunny. When did you arrive at Hitch's house?"

I leaned into the cushions, more relaxed than I had been for several hours. "I'll have to think back. We had a busy day at our grand opening, and I'm not sure of the exact time everything happened. I do remember that after we closed, Tilly left first—"

"Where'd she go?" he blurted out.

"Home, I suppose." Where *did* she go? Now, I wished she'd stayed with us at Shakes and Cakes. Isn't hindsight great?

He jotted down some notes and looked up, waiting for me to continue. "Tilly left first," he prompted.

"Right. Hitch and I sat down for a few minutes to let the day's go-go-go seep out of our systems. Then we checked that the kitties were all set for the night, locked up, and walked out. We were tired but feeling great about how well our grand opening went. And," I decided to add a personal touch, seeing as the

Chief seemed to be quite the kitty fan, "that little orange kitty you found? There are several people interested in adopting her. Isn't that great news?"

He nodded, but I wasn't sure if it had anything to do with the kitty or the other details about our day I'd just mentioned.

"Then you went to Hitch's house?"

"Before we left Shakes and Cakes, Officer Walker showed up."

A dark shadow passed over his face, disappearing so quickly I wouldn't have seen it if I hadn't been looking at him.

The Chief glanced toward the kitchen where we could still hear the murmur of voices. "What did he want? He was *supposed* to be interviewing the owner of the Bayside Bed and Breakfast and then report back to me."

"Mick said he'd found Ginger's phone. He wanted to know why she'd called Hitch, but he said he never answered the calls."

The Chief's face darkened. "Her *phone*? He's going behind my back with his own agenda, and I don't like it," he muttered as he pushed himself up from the chair. He placed Princess Muffin on the floor letting her decide where to finish her nap. "Thanks, Sunny."

Thanks? For what? I wasn't expecting that, but I'd take it.

"Officer Walker!" he hollered. "Time to go." He sounded fit to be tied. He was tired, probably hungry, and now angry. Not a good combination. For Mick.

Mick stomped out giving me a death glare if I'd ever seen one.

"What just happened?" Tilly asked when she and Hitch joined me to watch the two policemen drive away. "Mick was reading us the riot act, and I half expected him to cuff us and take us to the police station. Their quick exit makes no sense."

I scratched my head, suddenly exhausted. "Something's going on between those two and Mick has some explaining to do. The Chief has questions for him about Ginger's phone," I said and wondered what agenda Chief Bullock was referring to.

13

A rumble of thunder startled me from a deep sleep. It was *not* an encouraging start to the second day of business for Shakes and Cakes. Rain slashed at my windows, and Jasper whined next to my bed. Outside, clouds hovered over Pineville, leaving a dismal day underneath.

Princess Muffin and Stash remained curled together on my extra pillow like a four-legged, two-headed ball of gray, downy fur. The thunder didn't even make them twitch. Lucky them.

My nose twitched, though, as a rich aroma of strong dark coffee drifted into my room. My good fortune on a dreary day. Hitch, in a never-ending attempt to repair the damage to our relationship from when he up and left me for a job in New York

City, had made it his mission to spoil me rotten ever since he'd returned. I had zero plans to stop his efforts to arrive at my house early and have steaming coffee ready.

I slipped into clean jeans and a brand new white t-shirt, ran my comb through my hair, and swept it into a messy bun. Easy peasy.

A loud boom crashed right overhead, scaring a scream out of me.

"You okay up there, Sunshine?" Hitch called from the bottom of the stairs. "Coffee's ready."

Well, yeah, I could smell that. "Be right down."

Not wanting to spend another minute upstairs close to the thunder, I followed Jasper downstairs. The cheery kitchen and Hitch's easy smile helped me relax and feel safer.

To my surprise, Hitch didn't just have coffee ready. With a frilly pink apron tied around his waist, he poured eggs into a sizzling pan. "How does an omelet sound?" he asked.

I could get used to this treatment.

"Sounds like you heard my rumbling stomach over the storm. I am curious, though, to see you in my kitchen. I thought you'd stay and have coffee with your friend this morning. How'd you get in today? I *know* I didn't leave the door unlocked."

Hitch held up a key. "Had a copy made. Hope you don't mind. I left before my friend woke up." He glanced at me, but that twinkle in his eye made it impossible for me to even pretend to be annoyed.

Besides... omelet. I inhaled the buttery, cheesy, eggy delicious scent until my mouth watered. Between dropping the business partnership in my lap and feeding me, he'd figured out how to wiggle his way into my good graces.

I poured myself some coffee and leaned against the counter watching Hitch work. "Nice apron."

He looked down and lifted one corner as if he'd forgotten what he was wearing. "My mom's. I like to channel her when I'm in the kitchen. I might even let you borrow it sometime if you're nice to me."

Again, with the smile. It was too early in the morning to have tingles running through me but there was nothing I could do to stop them.

"No Tilly?" I asked, to distract myself from Hitch's charm. With her second sense of what was going on at my house, I expected her to arrive shortly for breakfast.

As if on cue, a loud rap sounded on the kitchen door. Even though I was expecting her, I still jumped and squeaked.

Hitch chuckled and folded the omelet in half.

"Amazing, right on time."

I yanked the door open, but it wasn't Tilly looking at me like a drowning rat.

"Can I come in?" Violet asked. She warily eyed Jasper as water dripped from umbrella to flowered rain boots.

"Um... sure." I stepped aside and motioned Jasper to sit.

Violet closed her umbrella and propped it next to the door before she came inside.

"I need your help." A puddle grew around her boots.

What could possibly cause Violet, my neighbor who didn't like me or my dog, to show up at my door, especially since it was barely past six in the morning?

I threw an old dishcloth on the puddle. "Do you want to sit down? Have some coffee?" I asked, not sure how I could help her.

Before Violet responded, my front door opened. "I smell coffee and eggs. I hope you made enough for me too, Hitch."

Tilly swept into the kitchen, spied Violet, and stopped short. She looked at me with eyebrows raised in two huge question marks.

Hitch, who somehow always seemed to keep his

cool, put two more mugs on the table and set two more places for breakfast. "Violet, take off your wet coat, and boots. Tilly, you insulted me with your comment. You know I always have enough for you. Now, all of you, sit down while I whip up more omelets."

And, just like that, the three of us sat at my table, waited on by the best looking guy in Pineville, and more importantly, the kindest man I knew. Without a hint of self-consciousness in his frilly pink apron, Hitch filled our mugs with coffee as if this morning was like any other. The fact that Violet fidgeted while she worked up her courage to share her problem made no difference to Hitch. He hummed to himself while he served each of us a perfectly browned omelet.

We dug in like we were starving. But it was more likely something to occupy us while we waited for Violet to unburden herself. No sense in letting Hitch's hard work go to waste.

Maybe it was his calm aura that filled my kitchen or maybe Violet finally had no option but to let her thoughts out, I'll never know. But she finally cleared her throat and began. "There's something I didn't tell the Chief yesterday."

Under the table, Tilly knocked her knee against

mine. I took it to mean, nothing wrong with that since we all held some secrets close to our chest.

Hitch pulled up a fourth chair and sat down between Violet and me. "Did you lie to him?" he asked as he sipped his coffee.

"Oh, no. I'd never lie. It's just that he never asked me if Ginger had a problem with any of us, including Greg, which could, you know, be a reason for murder."

"Did she?" Tilly asked. "Have problems with one of you?"

"Sort of," Violet said. She looked around my kitchen like she might find something that would help her through this difficulty. "I hate to betray a confidence. You see," she finally looked at us. "I'm older than the other girls. I started college after I'd worked for several years to save up money. They all kind of considered me to be more like a mother figure than their girlfriend. They shared their secrets with me because they knew I'd keep them locked away from the others."

Tilly put her coffee cup down and said, "That's all well and good but Ginger's dead." She was a little too blunt and sounded impatient. "Just spit out her secret, Violet."

But Violet took a deep breath and got to the

point. "Ginger didn't want Greg to come. She was adamant about that. I think once she found out he had decided to come with Carla, probably when she got to the Bayside Bed and Breakfast, that's when she did her disappearing act."

"Why didn't she want him to come?" I asked.

"Ginger and Greg had a quick fling. I really don't know all the details but I'm pretty sure that things didn't go according to Ginger's plan. Whatever happened, she was furious at Greg."

"So, why on earth would she plan this reunion? I mean, how could she spend time with Carla after something like that?" I asked.

"I don't have an answer for that question."

"But?" I asked, sensing there was more.

Violet was reluctant at first to tell us of her suspicions, but she was gathering steam. "I was worried she wanted to tell Carla to hurt Greg."

Hitch put his hand over Violet's. "Did Carla know about the affair?"

"I don't know, but my best guess is that, if she didn't know for sure, she had a strong suspicion. She keeps an eagle eye on Greg." She looked at Tilly and me. "You both saw how clingy she's been. And then you made that comment, Tilly, that maybe Greg and Ginger met up when he was picking up our dinner."

"I was only trying to get under her skin."

"I know, but I think it hit too close to home. Carla would do anything to keep Greg from leaving her."

I leaned toward Violet. "Do you think Carla murdered her to make sure that Ginger was definitely out of their lives? Or, maybe Greg killed her to protect his marriage?"

She looked up at the ceiling for a few moments before she answered. "Honestly, I don't know what to think but both of those possibilities did cross my mind." Violet pushed a few strands of wet hair off her cheek.

She shivered. Her shiver had nothing to do with being cold in my toasty warm kitchen. Violet's nerves were overloaded.

"How do you think we can help?" Hitch asked.

"Find out what happened to Ginger. She didn't deserve this," Violet said. A tear slid down her cheek. "Greg has always been a con man, and he can fool the best of the best. And, Carla acts a little ditzy, but she's sharp as a tack. As nice as Chief Bullock is, I don't think he's any match for either of them."

We had a crisis on our hands, a business to run, and kittens to take care of.

What a mess!

14

*O*nce Violet finished unloading her troubles on us, she sighed and asked for more coffee. She settled in comfortably like joining us for an early morning visit was her normal routine.

Far from it and now I had to figure out how to get rid of her.

"Violet?" I asked as I stood up and stacked our breakfast plates. "Thanks for coming over but we've got to head over to Shakes and Cakes. You know, it's time to open up for business."

"Oh, of course. I'll come with you. I just don't want to be alone right now. Maybe I can help?"

I froze. Did I hear her correctly?

Tilly patted Violet's hand. "Sure, Violet. You can

help Jasper with the kittens. How about you clean the litter boxes, feed them, and make sure they're clean from their bums to the tip of their noses? How does that sound?"

Jasper, hearing her name, lumbered to the table and nudged Violet's arm. She tensed and turned an unhealthy shade of gray. Was she about to faint? I put down the plates and prepared myself to grab her if she tumbled over.

But she stayed upright. "Oh," she said with little to none enthusiasm. "I thought I could maybe do some serving or mixing up the shakes and smoothies. I used to work as a waitress you know."

"That's a *wonderful* offer." Tilly sounded sincere to the untrained ear, but to me? I heard the sarcasm. "For now, Hitch and Sunny are behind the counter and I do the serving. I'm sure you understand." She even added a gentle pat on Violet's hand like they were best buddies.

Violet nodded. "Okay. It's high time I get over my fear of dogs, and Jasper does seem to like me. I'll help with the kittens.

What? Tilly and I locked on each other's shocked expression. This wasn't going as planned.

Violet patted Jasper on her head with her palm

flat as though she were afraid she would catch something. "Good doggie," she said and then she wiped her hands on a napkin. "That's settled then." She gave Tilly a worried smile. "I'll let the girls know where they can find me."

"You'll clean the litter boxes?" Tilly asked. Now, I was afraid *she* might faint.

Violet took a deep breath. "I will. I'm determined to help." She stood up, gave Jasper another tentative pat, and said, "I'll go change and meet you at Shakes and Cakes. You know?" She smiled broadly. "I'm looking forward to this. Thank you for making the offer so I can be of help."

We made the offer I thought as I watched her take off. She left with a bounce in her step that certainly wasn't there when she'd arrived. It appeared we'd acquired a new friend. Or at least, a tag-along like an annoying kid sister who won't go away even with a promise of a dollar.

"What the heck just happened?" Tilly asked as she stared at the door after Violet left. "That wasn't how she was supposed to react. Who in their right mind likes cleaning kitty litter boxes? I thought that would scare her away forever."

I chuckled at Tilly's reaction. She wasn't used to

having her clever manipulations backfire. If I didn't know better, I'd say Violet just gave Tilly a dose of her own medicine.

"Look at it this way," I said. "Violet and her girlfriends will be right under our noses. With everything that happened, now, we can find out more details about their relationships. I doubt Carla will let Greg out of her sight for more than a nanosecond, so he's the one I plan to focus on first. Where else did he go yesterday and who did he go with?"

Hitch rubbed his hands together. "I for one like a challenge, and I think Violet just manipulated us right into her corner to help find Ginger's killer. And, we didn't even see it coming. We'd better keep an eye on *her*. After all, she seems to know more about Ginger than the others. Maybe *she* has a dark secret that Ginger planned to reveal."

I put the rest of the dishes in the sink and rinsed them quickly to finish up later. "I never thought of that, Hitch," I said, drying my hands on a dish towel. "I bet each one of them has a secret. If Ginger had a stalker, and she wanted to hire you to guard her, somehow we have to figure out who that stalker was."

"Greg," Tilly said with total confidence. "Or, Carla," she added. "They've been married since college, right? He had a little fun on the side according to Violet, but it doesn't mean the marriage was over. Was either one desperate enough to silence her?"

"Or, they worked together," Hitch said.

"Don't forget Laura who likes to sit back and stay under the radar," I said. "Those quiet types

I picked up my bag and dropped in some lotion and lip balm plus some dog bones for Jasper while I considered Tilly's question. "From what we know now, if it's all true, Greg had the opportunity, the motive, and possibly the means. And maybe Carla helped by distracting the others."

"Exactly," Tilly said. "If Ginger was poisoned like Hitch suspects, we have to figure out who poisoned her. Maybe something lethal was added to the smoothie I left on the counter."

As soon as those words left Tilly's mouth, she blanched. "That sounds so much worse out loud than when it was still just in my head. If someone poisoned that smoothie, and it gets tied back to me..."

We all stood still. Nobody said a word. What was there to say? Tilly had just said it all. The circle of evidence came right back to her.

Now we had to figure out who had access to that

smoothie besides Tilly. And more important: where did the poison come from?

"Come on Jasper," I said to break the tension in the kitchen. "We have kittens to feed and customers to help." At least *that* was something I could get my head wrapped around. I slipped into my raincoat even though the rain had let up. A thick fog from Blueberry Bay enveloped Pineville and would most likely last through the morning.

I drove with Hitch and Tilly followed us in her new Volkswagen bug. When I say followed, she was practically on our back bumper every time I turned around to look.

"Speed up, Hitch. We need more space between your car and hers. The next thing we know, she'll get distracted and ram right into us. That's the last thing we need this morning."

Hitch sped up and timed running the yellow light perfectly. We got through but Tilly had to slam on her brakes or risk a ticket. For once, some common sense prevailed.

"Phew!" I wiped my brow. "It's barely seven o'clock and I feel like I've already lived a weeks' worth of problems and dodged several bullets."

Hitch patted my thigh. "Don't worry so much,

Sunshine. You won't have time to think about Ginger's murder today. We'll be too busy focusing on shakes and cakes and adorable kittens.

I hoped Hitch was right.

But I was worried he wasn't.

15

Excitement replaced my anxiety as soon as I spotted our Shakes and Cakes sign. I'd been worried that the drama-filled morning had sapped all my energy.

When Hitch pulled into the parking lot, all the red, orange, and yellow blooms filling our pots and hanging baskets lit up the gray day like a string of bright lights. A welcome sight if I'd ever seen one.

I stood outside the car, admiring our hard work. So worth it. Instead of a vacant building and empty greenhouse, a welcoming destination beckoned the public. They just had to walk through the gate and dip under the arch to experience a world filled with beauty. The variety of delicious treats inside was the next surprise. Oh, and kittens to cuddle.

I smiled and Hitch jostled me with his elbow.

"What's the smile for, Sunshine?"

"This." I waved my arm to take in what we'd built. "It really makes me happy."

Tilly rumbled in behind us and swerved into a parking spot. "Quick!" she said after she'd jumped out of her car and jogged toward us. "I think Officer Walker is on his way here. You two go inside, and I'll try to distract him."

By distract, she meant get rid of. Fine by me.

My happiness evaporated like a popped soap bubble as I hurried toward the door where Jasper waited, not so patiently. She knew the routine and was anxious to check on her kitties.

"I'll get started with the fruit prep for smoothies if you want to help Jasper count kittens," Hitch said. I think he really just wanted me as far away from Mick as possible, so I didn't fall back into my gloomy mood. Again, fine with me and with a tiny bit of luck, I wouldn't even see him.

After I checked Mama Cat and her kittens, I picked up the newest addition, the adorable orange kitty, Clawdia, and gave her a snuggle. "How are you doing today?"

She batted my cheek and mewed.

"Is that right?" I said to Clawdia before I set her

down so Jasper could get busy with her own style of inspection.

"Fresh water and food and you'll be all set, right?"

Mama Cat wound around my legs, practically tripping me as I filled all the bowls. One of her kittens jumped off a shelf onto my back when I was bent over. As the kitten walked across my shoulders, the four little feet felt like a gentle massage. A ticklish massage.

I laughed.

"Sunny? Do you need some help?"

I felt the weight of the kitten disappear off my back, and I straightened up.

"Dani?" Emotion overwhelmed me as I hugged my friend from Misty Harbor. Dani Mackenzie had been there for me when a few months earlier, Jasper towed me out of the ice-cold water of Blueberry Bay. Dani kept me safe when a killer wanted to silence me.

"Hey," Dani held me at arm's length and looked at me. Her mass of auburn curls spilled from her hair clips as tears spilled from my eyes.

"What's wrong, Sunny?"

I wiped my eyes with my palms and said, "Sorry.

There's been so much going on, I guess I finally lost control."

"Well, I'm glad I decided to make the cupcake run over here today. I get to see you and your new place."

She looked around the greenhouse while I pulled myself together. Seeing my friend helped bring the sunshine back to my spirit.

"This jungle of plants and kittens is incredible, Sunny. Who was that little fur ball I took off your back?"

"Razzleberry." I lifted the kitten up to our eye level. "Cute, right? But a bit of a troublemaker."

"They *all* are in my experience, right Pip?"

Dani's Jack Russel terrier yipped her agreement. At least that was *my* interpretation.

"Hey there, Pip." After I'd crouched down to give the little dog my undivided attention, I returned my focus to Dani. "Everything's all set in here. Jasper keeps an eye on the kitties. Do you have time for me to whip up a smoothie for you while Pip helps Jasper here?"

"I'd love that. Today's my day off. My employees at the Little Dog Diner have everything under control. My whole day is open. Do you need help here?"

"Not at the moment," I said knowing that things could change quickly. I led the way into the shop. I could tell that Dani was worried about me, and I appreciated the offer to help. I peeked through the front window as I ushered Dani to the counter. Officer Walker was still outside in the parking lot with Tilly. That was a relief. "What would you like, Dani?"

She glanced at the blackboard above us. "How about that mango, blueberry fruit smoothie?"

"Coming right up," I said, tying my apron on and getting the ingredients from the fridge. Hitch had stacked and labeled everything clearly, so I had no problem whipping up my friend's drink. Where was Hitch? I wondered.

As if reading my mind, Hitch and Conrad walked in from the side door, chatting and laughing.

"Hey, Sunshine," Hitch said after greeting Dani. "Conrad offered to make tables for outside along the front of the shop. What do you think about that idea?"

"I think," I said and grinned at Conrad, "that Mr. Tough Guy will do anything so he can stop by to visit the kittens. Am I right?"

I handed Dani her smoothie and she leaned

against the counter, settling in to observe our interaction.

Conrad looked away like he was embarrassed. "You got me there, Sunny. Your little fur balls are irresistible. I decided to stop by so they don't forget who I am. Do you need me to hang around with them today? You know, to help Jasper?" He sounded like he wouldn't mind one bit if I asked him to stay, but I suspected he had places to be and jobs to do.

"Actually, my neighbor, Violet Burnham—"

"She's your neighbor?" Conrad asked like I lived next to a serial killer.

"You know her?"

"Unfortunately." He looked around as if expecting someone to eavesdrop. "She hired me to build a patio for her and never paid. Not one cent. And, on top of that, she bad-mouthed me to everyone she knew. Claimed I did shoddy work, and she had to hire someone else to finish what I started. It was all lies."

I couldn't believe it. I'd never been particularly fond of Violet, but I'd chalked it up to her dislike of Jasper. Maybe I'd been lucky to have avoided her until this morning.

"I'd dodge her like the plague if I were you," he added.

"It's too late for that. She volunteered to clean the kitty litter boxes and help Jasper watch the kittens today. I hope I didn't make a huge mistake by letting her help out."

I had a picture of her arriving at my kitchen door this morning during the pouring rain. She seemed genuinely upset.

Was it possible that she had an ulterior motive when she'd stopped in?

16

Conrad offered his hand to Dani. "I don't think we've met. I'm Conrad Coleman, from Misty Harbor."

Dani shook it and said, "Small world, Mr. Coleman. I'm Dani Mackenzie, owner of the Little Dog Diner. I think you know my husband, Luke."

Conrad smacked the side of his head. "Of course. I thought you looked familiar. What brings you to Pineville?" He nodded at the drink in Dani's hand. "Besides the smoothies, of course. And, the kittens." He grinned like this was our ongoing joke.

"A cupcake delivery," Dani said. "Plus, I wanted to see how Sunny and Hitch had transformed the old Nine Pine Nursery into this Shakes and Cakes business." She nodded at me approvingly. "I missed the grand opening yesterday, but I'm sure you were swamped and wouldn't have had time to visit with me anyway."

"It *was* busy," I said. "And, it didn't help that we were the last people to see the woman who was murdered."

"Another murder?" Dani's blue eyes grew into saucer-shaped spheres. "Not here I hope."

"Not here," Hitch said. "But the victim stopped in before she disappeared into thin air."

"And her body was found in Hitch's apartment kitchen," I added. I nodded toward the parking lot and grimaced. "Officer Walker, out there, has been giving us a lot of grief, but Tilly seems to have him under control for now." By under control, I meant out of our shop.

As we watched, Officer Walker spun Tilly around and cuffed her.

"Oh no!" I yelped and rushed outside.

"What are you doing?" I hollered

Officer Walker pointed his finger at me. "You'll be next if you don't watch your step."

I had no idea what *that* was supposed to mean but I did know I wouldn't abandon Tilly.

Before Mick had Tilly in the back of the police car, she yelled, "Hitch's sexy neighbor said that she saw me go into his apartment and never come out again. Sunny, do something!"

An adrenaline surge had me shaking from head to toe. Hitch put his arm around my shoulders and pulled me close, anchoring me before I ran after the police car with my fist raised.

This had just escalated from horrible to catastrophic. Tilly was in a heap of trouble.

Dani came up to me. "I know a good lawyer. Want me to call?"

I looked at Dani, then Hitch. "What should we do?"

"Not yet," Hitch said. "Someone needs to go talk to my neighbor."

"Exactly what I was thinking." I said, already preparing a story to get in the door. "I'll go talk to her. I'll pretend to be the victim's friend or something like that. You need to stay here, Hitch."

Jasper came up and wagged her tail as if to bolster my spirits.

"Pip and I will go with you, Sunny," Dani said. "We'll get that neighbor talking and she won't know what hit her."

Hitch paced back and forth a few steps. It wasn't like my laid-back partner to show anxiety. "What about Shakes and Cakes? We have to open in about a half hour," he said, "I'm not sure I can juggle all this on my own. At least not efficiently."

"I'll help you here," Conrad said, giving Hitch one of those man slaps on his back. "Give me one of those hot pink aprons, and I can serve the donuts and cupcakes like a champ."

Violet, who'd dropped completely off my radar, pulled into the parking lot. I was actually happy to see her. As good as Jasper was as the Chief Kitty Nanny, she couldn't answer questions or take down the information about potential adopters.

I pulled Hitch, Conrad, and Violet inside. I reminded Hitch where to find the various recipes, and he was good to go. All Conrad had to do was serve whatever pastry the customer wanted. Easy peasy. Violet, on the other hand, needed a little more guidance. In the greenhouse, she listened carefully and got right to cleaning the litter boxes without any complaining.

"Ready?" Dani asked when I returned to the shop.

"Let's do this," I said, with more bravado than real confidence.

Dani clipped on Pip's leash. "My girl Pip is a great ice breaker and not quite as intimidating as Jasper. I mean... I don't mean that Jasper is intimidating to *me*, but she is big. And you know, that can scare some people."

Dani's fumbling around to make sure she didn't insult Jasper almost had me laughing. If the situation wasn't so serious, I would have given her a hard time. Under the circumstances, though, I held my hand up. "I know what you mean. Pip is a great asset to have along. Besides, Jasper's work is cut out for her here. She has to keep Violet in line."

Conrad rolled his eyes. "I'll be sure to help Jasper with *that* job when I can. Now, get going. Times a wasting. And, let's hope that Tilly doesn't turn into a caged tiger at the police station."

"Knowing Tilly," I said as I grabbed my bag, "the police will be thankful when they finally get rid of *her*."

Hitch let out a snort. "I wouldn't be surprised to hear that Tilly locked everyone in a cell and convinced them it was for their own safety."

I wasn't going to dawdle waiting for *that* to happen, but the image did make me chuckle.

I headed to Dani's dark green MG. "You drive, Dani. I came with Hitch this morning."

"I hope you don't mind riding with Pip on your lap. As far as she's concerned, the passenger seat belongs to her, but she'll share."

We settled in her car and Dani pulled out of the parking lot. With the top down, it would be a windy ride this morning. "Back toward town?"

"Yup."

Pip had her front paws on the dash as she watched everything zip by.

"Tell me about Hitch's neighbor," Dani said.

"I've never met her, but Hitch pointed her out to me once. Ashley Mulford is attractive, mid-twenties, and according to Hitch, she managed to bump into him several times a day after he returned to Pineville. He said she'd giggle and touch his arm, all flirty like."

Dani gave me a quick glance and raised her eyebrows. "So, she likes Hitch? Why would she embellish her story to get *Tilly* in trouble?"

Why? I wasn't sure, but I could make a fairly good guess. "Tilly goes to Hitch's apartment quite often to take him muffins or some other tasty treat in the mornings. Knowing Tilly, I suspect she told Ashley to mind her own business and leave Hitch alone. And, not tactfully. Tilly's not known to mince words."

"Turn here," I said pointing to Hitch's street. "Here's my plan. We'll say we were Ginger's friends, and we just want to find out what happened to her.

You know, we'll be all weepy and distraught. Can you do that?"

"No problem, but what if Ashley recognizes you?"

"I'll just have to take that risk. The only time I went to Hitch's apartment was yesterday, and I'm hoping she didn't see me with him. Park here. That's his apartment."

And, it was my lucky day. Ashley was walking up the path to the front door.

"Excuse me!" I called from the open window.

Ashley stopped and smiled at us, showing bright white teeth against a dark tan and bleached blonde hair. "Can I help you?" She walked toward the MG.

"I hope so." I opened the door, letting Pip jump out first.

"We're Ginger's friends. I heard this is where the police," I paused and wiped my eye. In a whisper I said, "Where they found her. Do you live here?" I asked, hoping my face held an appropriate amount of concern and sadness.

Ashley took a quick glance at Pip sniffing her shoes, but otherwise ignored her. "The dead woman? Really? Like, you knew her? How horrible! Yes, I live here, but I think the police arrested the killer. You know, *I* saw her go into Mr. Hitchner's apartment."

Ashley's face flushed. Was it from excitement? My stomach twisted in a knot, rendering me speechless.

Dani came to my rescue and saved me from my temporary silence. "What happened?" she asked breathlessly.

"Come in, and I'll tell you everything," she said like we were all co-conspirators. "Officer Walker didn't tell me to keep anything to myself."

She was much too excited about what she claimed to know.

What did that mean?

17

Ashley led the way to her apartment right next to Hitch's and opened the door for us.

Inside, she dropped her bag and shrugged out of her light jacket. Pip bolted ahead and wasted no time sniffing around the room.

I glanced around behind Ashley. The layout matched Hitch's apartment, but the atmosphere felt like a dungeon instead of his bright cheery space. Her curtains were closed, the furniture was crowded together, and the walls were covered with dark posters.

What had Dani and I walk into?

"So," Ashley said, as she plopped onto a black chair, crossed her legs, and looked like someone ready to share some juicy gossip. All she needed was a bowl of popcorn and a cold drink to make the scene complete. "Sit down and tell me about your friend."

Since Dani had never met Ginger, I jumped in. "It's hard to talk about her," I said, adding a sniffle for effect. "You know, we just planned to have a fun weekend." I scooched to the edge of my chair. "Did you actually see her?"

Pip finished exploring and jumped onto Dani's lap. Ashley recoiled and said, "Is your dog, like, housetrained? I don't want any piddles on my floor."

"No worries," Dani said. "Pip goes everywhere with me and never has an accident. It's interesting," she added, "Pip kind of adopted me after her previous owner was murdered."

Ashley's mouth fell open. "That's just creepy. Kind of like what I heard when I was in my kitchen. You know, it's only separated from Hitch's kitchen by a wall, and you wouldn't believe what I hear. I don't think he knows that." She smirked.

What else did she hear from Hitch's kitchen? Talk about creepy. Ashley held the medal for that title in my opinion.

"So, anyway," she said flapping her hands around like little windmills. "It was like I had people right in here with me when that woman in Hitch's kitchen screamed. 'what are you doing here?' Of course, I stopped getting my snack ready and listened. Who wouldn't?"

"And that woman was Ginger?" I asked.

Ashley sat back with a satisfied expression. "It must have been."

"Who was she talking to?"

"Well," she sat forward again. "This is the interesting part. I saw Tilly Morris, an old busybody in town, let herself into Hitch's apartment." She paused to look at Dani, then me. "And I never saw her leave. I think she was, like, hiding inside waiting to kill that woman."

"You *think*?" I said.

"Well, it makes sense. I saw her go in. A while later I heard the scream. It doesn't take a detective to put all *that* together."

Well, actually it *does* take a lot of detective work to put facts together. Concrete evidence, not thoughts and assumptions. But apparently, Ashley wasn't concerned about *those* minor details.

"You told all that to Officer Walker, just like you told us?" I asked.

"Pretty much. What do you think? You guys were Ginger's friends."

Oh right, I'd forgotten about our little charade. "I

wonder what the motive for murder was. I mean, if this Tilly person *was* still in the house," I let that thought hang in the air for several long seconds, "how did she even know Ginger was coming? And, why would she kill her?"

Ashley flicked her hand through the air. "Those are the details for the police to figure out."

Oh right, those pesky little details.

"Where were you when you saw Tilly go into Mr. Hitchner's apartment?" I asked wondering if anything Ashley said was backed by anything real.

"Oh, I'd just gotten home from work and was parking when I saw Tilly walking to the door. She was inside before I got out of my car."

I pointed to the curtained view. "And once you were inside, you watched through your window the whole time to see if anyone went in or out until you heard the scream?"

"Well, not the *whole* time. I went into the kitchen to fix myself a snack. And, it's a good thing I did, or I wouldn't have heard the scream."

I nodded and looked at Dani. A quick twitch of her eyebrows back at me made me assume she thought Ashley's story was as full of holes as I did. Why then did Officer Walker cuff Tilly and take her to the police station?

I stood up. "Thanks, Ashley. This has been helpful in this difficult time." I sniffled again and hoped it didn't sound too fake to her.

"I only wish I'd been able to help your friend, but I was too afraid to barge in."

"How would you have helped? Do you have a gun or something like that?" I asked.

"Oh, no, I'm afraid of guns." She giggled like a preteen. "I've never told anyone else this, but I have a knack for accidentally on purpose bumping into Hitch. I kind of like him, and I like to see him and talk to him whenever I can. I wonder now, if I'd bumped into Tilly, maybe she would have changed her mind and not gone inside. And then that poor woman would be alive now."

Okay. Ashley sounded more and more like a stalker. I doubted there was anything true about her story except maybe she did see Tilly go inside. But, the rest? I'd bet my new business that it was all fabricated by an obsessed woman looking for attention. Most likely, Hitch's attention.

"I'm curious, Ashley," I said. "Did you see Mr. Hitchner when he got home? He found the body, didn't he?"

"I'm kicking myself that I decided to take a shower and ended up missing *all* the excitement. By the time I stepped out of my shower and got dressed, the police were in his apartment. I don't know where he was. I never saw him come home or leave."

Ashley was a completely unreliable witness, so why did Mick take Tilly to the police station?

"Thanks for your time. We can let ourselves out."

I knew it sounded abrupt, but I couldn't get away from her fast enough. Unfortunately, she walked us to the door. When she put her hand on my arm, my skin tingled like I'd reached into a patch of stinging nettles.

"Do you think I'm safe here?" Ashley asked. "What if there's not enough evidence to keep that murderer locked up? Do you think she'll come here and kill me if she finds out I heard that stuff through the wall?"

"First, Ashley, everyone is innocent until proven guilty so I'm not sure that the person you've accused is the murderer."

Ashley's mouth fell open. "You don't believe me?"

"Let's put it this way. There are a few gaps in your story. But I do believe you heard *something* and that does put you in danger. You should *absolutely* be concerned that you could be a target. If the killer finds out that you've been blabbing about hearing what you claim you've heard, you're in serious danger."

I pulled my arm away from her claw-like grip.

Her eyes narrowed like something had just clicked in her brain. "You aren't really Ginger's friends, are you? I've seen you around town. Why did you come here?"

"We're looking for the truth, Ashley. And the killer. And you'd better hope someone finds that person before they find you."

Dani, Pip, and I walked out. I heard the distinct sound of the door slamming closed and the lock clicking.

"That was harsh, Sunny. But I think you're right about her being in trouble."

I slid onto the passenger seat of Dani's MG, patted my lap, and waited for Pip to settle in. When Dani pulled away from the curb, I said, "It doesn't matter what we think. It's what the killer believes that puts Ashley in danger."

"True. It's shocking that she never considered that angle. I wonder what she'll do now."

I had a pretty good idea. She'd play on Hitch's good nature and ask him to protect her.

18

"Dani, do you have time to swing by the police station?" I asked as we moved into traffic. "After listening to Ashley's ridiculous account of what she *thinks* happened, I want to find out what's going on with Tilly. It doesn't sound like Mick has much of anything to keep her."

Dani grinned at me like a co-conspirator. "You read my mind. I've got all day to help you track down leads if that's your plan and you want my help," she said. "Pip and I have done stuff like this a few times before, don't forget."

Looking at Dani Mackenzie, with her mass of auburn curls cascading around her face, I was reminded of exactly how clever she was when she'd rescued me. I couldn't be luckier to have her at my side when Hitch and I worked on any sleuthing activities.

Dani reached over and fluffed Pip's ears. "What do you think, Pipster? You did some sniffing around Ashley's apartment. Did you find anything interesting?"

Pip yipped and wagged her tail.

"Right," Dani said. "No kitty or doggy odors for you to investigate. I don't think Ashley will be stopping at your Kitty Castle to adopt one of the fur balls. But I wouldn't count her out of stopping in to cause trouble."

I straightened Pip's lavender bandana which, ironically, was covered with kittens. "I have a strict adoption application, then a home visit before *any* kitten leaves my care. Ashley definitely does not fit the bill even if she wanted one of the kittens. I mean, it was a dungeon in her apartment. Do you think she ever opens the curtains?"

Dani tossed me a side-eye before returning her concentration to the road. "I think she likes to spy on her neighbor, and it works better if she keeps the curtains open just a crack for her spying. Are you going to let Hitch know about her obsession?"

"You have to ask? Of course, I will! He's not a fan of her anyway, and maybe now he'll keep as far away as possible."

Dani nudged my arm. "He's awfully handsome with those green eyes and chiseled jaw."

I felt my cheeks heat up. I suspected that Dani had seen enough to know that Hitch and I had a complicated relationship. Heck, I couldn't even understand it, so how could she?

"Don't worry, I'm not going to grill you about what is or isn't going on between you and Hitch. I'm just saying I think he's a great friend and business partner for you. If it turns into something else? Don't fight it." She grinned at me knowingly. "Now, where's the police station?"

Oh, right, I'd spaced out thinking about Hitch. "Turn left here and you'll see it up ahead."

Dani zipped around the corner forcing me to catch Pip as she lost her balance and fell into my lap.

"Sorry, Pipsqueak. Crazy driver at the wheel," Dani said like she was enjoying this whole adventure.

I pointed to the police station. "There! And there's Tilly, looking fresh as a daisy. I don't know why I ever worry about her. She can talk her way out of a paper bag or getting locked up. Whichever comes first. Is she waiting for a ride?"

Dani screeched to a stop. I jammed one hand on the dashboard, bracing myself as I tightened my hold on Pip.

"Well, *someone* has ESP." Tilly said as she gave a little wave and put her phone away. "I didn't even make a call yet." She opened the door and looked at the cramped space behind the MG's seats. "You expect me to squish in *there*? My stuffed teddy bear would be cramped."

"What? You love to brag about what good shape you're in," I said forcing myself to keep a straight face but knowing I'd lose this argument.

"I don't think so, Sunny. I'm seventy and you're what? Barely thirty? *You* get in the back, and I'll sit up front with the Pipsqueak."

Pip jumped out, and I huffed and rolled my eyes like I was extremely put out, but Dani and Tilly only laughed at me.

"Quit with the drama queen act, Sunny. It doesn't suit you at all," Tilly said once I'd stuffed myself sideways into the space meant for a small suitcase and not a hundred-and-twenty-pound female. After she was comfortable in the passenger seat with Pip,

Tilly tightened her scarf around her hair and looked at Dani. "Ready to roll. Show me what this sports car of yours can do."

Dani laughed, and I silently prayed that we'd make it safely back to Shakes and Cakes. Why did I put my life in the hands of these women who pretended they were driving on a racetrack?

"I can't risk getting pulled over," Dani said. "I think I've used up all my warnings."

That gave me a little bit of relief that I wasn't about to become a statistic in the next fifteen minutes. She did, however, leave the parking lot with enough spin of the tires that Tilly raised her arms and shouted with glee.

"Freedom!"

I leaned between the two front seats hoping to get to the reason for Tilly's trip to the police station. "What happened? Why did Mick cuff you?"

Tilly leaned sideways and said over her shoulder, "That man is a fool. The problem was that I told him and, big surprise, he didn't like it. What can I say? Truth hurts." She shrugged as if her trip to the pokey was just a little blip in her day. "And then, when I put my hands on his chest and blocked him from going into Shakes and Cakes, you should have seen his face, Sunny. It almost burst into a million pieces. He managed to hiss that I'd gone too far. Hey, I only wanted to keep him from becoming a big nuisance while you were trying to get ready to open for business. It worked, too."

"Thanks?" Was I glad about what she'd done or should I worry about her rogue tendencies? Not like I had a say in the matter.

"The best part of being at the police station," Tilly said, looking me in the eye. She probably was afraid I'd tuned her out, but she had my attention. "I overheard some interesting conversations about Ginger's murder. Mind you, it was only snippets here and there, but I heard Carla's husband, Greg's name mentioned several times. I don't know what it means, but I know his behavior set off *my* alarm bells and apparently he is now on the police radar as a person of interest."

"Dani and I talked to Hitch's neighbor, Ashley." I said, thinking about alarm bells.

"Oh, I forgot all about her. That was the *official* reason Mick used to take me to the police station. He said she'd identified me going into Hitch's house. What did she tell you two?"

"A story full of holes." I shifted as much as

possible in my cramped space but nothing I did made me more comfortable. "I believe that she saw you go inside but she really wasn't paying attention to anyone going in or out after that. She made a snack in her kitchen and took a shower so anything could have happened. She did say that she heard someone scream, 'What are you doing here?' That's possibly true, but who was it? While Greg was driving to the Little Dog Diner, he said he saw Ginger walking on the side of the road. Did he follow her?"

Dani's head whipped around to look at me. "This person of interest was at the Little Dog Diner yesterday? It was so busy, I probably wouldn't remember even if I'd seen him."

She turned into the Shakes and Cakes parking lot. "I'm still trying to figure out how Ginger got into Hitch's apartment in the first place."

"I don't know," I said. "But, when Hitch and I got to his apartment, the door was unlocked. Very unlike Hitch to forget to lock up."

"Maybe I forgot to lock it when I left," Tilly said. "I've done that before."

"So, here's what we have." I ticked off the series of events. "Tilly went to Hitch's apartment. Ashley saw her go in, When Tilly left, she forgot to lock the door. Ginger walked to Hitch's apartment and let herself in. Ashley saw her go in." I looked at Dani and Tilly.

"With the door unlocked, anyone could have followed her inside," I said.

19

I waited for Tilly to get out of Dani's car before I managed to unfold my body enough to squeeze myself out on to the sidewalk. It took a lot of grunts and groans, but I finally stretched all the kinks out.

"Geesh, Sunny," Tilly said, "you sound like an old lady."

I gave her a nasty glare. "Next time it's you back there if you think it's so comfy."

Hitch saw us and jogged over. He pushed some stray hairs out of my face and tucked them behind my ears. "You look a little windblown. Did you have a nice ride in Dani's convertible?"

Tilly snorted. "Sunny's a little ornery since she

was in that back space. You might want to give her some time to cool off."

To his credit, he put his arm around my shoulder and gave me a hug. I rested in the crook of his strong arm and inhaled an aroma of chocolate mixed with coffee. Yum. If a ride squished in the back of Dani's MG got me this kind of extra attention from Hitch, I'd do it again without complaining.

Tilly brushed her fingers through her wind-blown hair and fixed her scarf back in place. "Hitch," she said before I had a chance to query him, "what's happened around here since I got carted away?"

Before he answered, Hitch whispered, "I'm glad you're back." His breath tickled my neck, and I shivered delightfully. He turned to Tilly. "It's been wild. Violet's girlfriends showed up and parked themselves in the greenhouse with her. I don't know how much attention they actually paid to the kittens, but Conrad checked occasionally and said everything seemed fine. Greg arrived about a half hour ago, and he's been sitting by himself in the corner of the shop, staring at nothing."

"Carla let him sit alone?" I asked, assuming she'd have a tighter grip on him now more than ever.

"Well, she comes out every five minutes and tries to sweet talk him, but he just grumbles something I can't hear, and she goes back to the greenhouse looking like a whipped puppy."

I was glad to see people leaving Shakes and Cakes with bags of pastries, tall drink cups, and beautiful orchids while more customers arrived and went inside. Regardless of the drama playing out behind the scenes, our business continued as if everything was normal.

"Ready to go inside, Sunshine?" Hitch asked. "I told Conrad I'd be right back."

"You bet I am, and the first thing I plan to do is talk to Greg. Tilly said she heard his name mentioned several times while she was in the police station." I looked at Tilly and Dani. "Can you two help Hitch for a bit?"

"Of course," they both said as one.

Once we got inside, I headed straight for Greg. I didn't expect an invitation to join him, so I pulled out a chair and sat down. His shirt was wrinkled, and he hadn't shaved. But worse than that was the blank expression around his red-rimmed eyes.

"Greg," I said and tapped my finger on his arm.

He lifted his eyes to meet mine like it was the hardest movement he'd ever made. "You know," he said. "I should have stopped and given Ginger a ride yesterday when I saw her on the road."

I patted his hand like we were friends, even though I wasn't even sure if he remembered seeing me at Violet's house yesterday. "How could you have known what was going to happen." Or, did he?

"I suppose that's true, but I'm also not surprised."

My heart beat faster as I wondered where this conversation was going. Was he about to confess to something? I looked around our shop. I was glad people were close by, and I wasn't alone with this man. He seemed to be holding some dark secret.

"Why?" I asked.

"Ginger is... was..." he dropped his head onto his hands.

"Ginger was what?"

He lifted his head, his steely eyes boring into me. He let out a kind of manic sound. "She was someone with the kind of personality that could pull you close. Do you know what I mean?"

I nodded, not sure I did but wanting him to continue.

"Then boom." He slammed his hand on the table. I jumped. "She'd discard you like a piece of trash."

I didn't have to ask if he was talking about himself; it was more than obvious. Instead, I said, "Ginger came here yesterday morning looking for protection. Do you have any idea who she was afraid of?"

"She came here? You knew her?" His eyes closed into suspicious slits.

"No, I never met her before, but she'd met my partner in New York. She wanted his help."

I heard footsteps approaching.

"Greg! Pull yourself together." Carla stood, with her hands on her hips, glaring at her husband. "You're acting like you lost your best friend when we all know that Ginger didn't want anything to do with you. Now, this may sound harsh, but we don't want to just sit around moping all day, so we've decided to still go on the Blueberry Bay boat tour and you're coming with us."

Greg pushed himself off his chair. "You've decided you don't want to sit around and mope? My goodness *that* shows Ginger the respect she deserves. But, why am I surprised? You all pretended to like each other when in reality you couldn't wait to gossip and throw knives at each other's backs as fast as you could pick them up."

Was it my imagination, or did Carla stamp her foot? "I don't know what's gotten into you, Greg. I know you and Ginger were close in the past, but that was years ago."

"Listen, Carla," he sneered. "I didn't want to come this weekend. You nagged and said it would be a nice romantic weekend for us. You made me feel guilty. A romantic weekend? Ha. What a joke. All you do is giggle and preen and watch my every move. I don't want anything to do with you *or* your girlfriends. I'm going to get my stuff from the Bayside Bed and Breakfast and I'll find another place to stay." He stepped around her and walked out.

Awkward!

Carla stood frozen in place. Her mouth hung open as red bloomed from her neck to her forehead. Was she embarrassed or angry?

"I'm gonna kill him," she muttered.

I put my money on embarrassed and hoped she wasn't serious about the killing part.

But what did I know?

Did Greg need to be warned?

20

Carla looked at me, all remnants of her normally bubbly manner long gone. "What are *you* staring at?"

"Are you okay?" I asked, ignoring her hostility.

"Of course, I'm not okay." She scanned the shop area, to cool down I think, "My friend is dead. My husband just walked out on me and, I'm afraid he might be a murderer."

"Because he said he passed Ginger walking while on his way to Misty Harbor yesterday?"

"Forget what I just said about Greg. I didn't mean it." Carla glared at me and jabbed her finger in my face, making her curls bob around her head like a caricature of Shirley Temple. It was hard to take her seriously. "Violet was right. You and your friend, that old busy body, are nothing but trouble. I heard she was arrested. How come she's here and not in jail? Is she looking for her next victim?"

"Is there a problem here?" I felt Hitch's hands on my shoulders as he stood behind me. It was a relief to know that someone so strong and capable had my back.

"And, who are you?" Carla's whole demeanor changed in a flash to a flirty female out to woo a handsome hunk. She held her hand out and winked. "Carla Singleton."

Hitch shook her hand. "Ty Hitchner. Could I tempt you—"

"You certainly could, Mr. Hitchner. Ginger told us about her handsome friend from New York." She giggled. "But I suspected that she was exaggerating. Just the opposite." She scanned Hitch from head to toe. Slowly.

What a Jekyll and Hyde performance I thought as I watched this two-faced woman make a fool out of herself.

Hitch pulled his hand away from Carla's. "I was going to say, tempt you with one of our shakes."

Her eyes narrowed. I think it finally registered in her small brain that Hitch's hand was on *my* shoulder. She must have put two and two together, realizing that Hitch was my business partner and not some random handsome customer swooping in to be her knight in shining armor.

"I don't think so," she said, her flirty smile turning sour. "I wouldn't trust anything you people serve. Violet told us that Ginger came here looking for you. But I didn't know you were connected to *her*." She pointed to me with an accusatory scowl. "For all we know, you put something in Ginger's drink. Have the police looked into *that*?"

"I'm curious, Carla," I said, not taking my eyes off her face. "What were *you* doing before you showed up at Violet's house last night? You girls had reservations at the Bayside Bed and Breakfast. It's not much of a drive or walk, for that matter, to get from there to Hitch's apartment where Ginger's body was found." I tapped my finger on my lips like I was figuring something out. "I think that you had a big problem with Ginger's relationship with your husband. Maybe *that's* something the police need to look into."

"I never," she said as rage filled her face. "My husband loves me."

"Really. He sure has an interesting way of showing it. As a matter of fact, I got the complete *opposite* impression when he stomped out of here,

Carla. And, according to your girlfriend, Laura, Ginger was a big flirt. Greg's a handsome guy. Hmmm, it doesn't take much of a leap to add those two things together and imagine a connection between Greg and Ginger."

Her hands flapped. Was she trying to fly away from my probing? "Well, Greg's the one with some explaining to do, then. Don't try to pin this murder on *me*. He had the car. He was gone for a couple of hours to who knows where. I was at the bed and breakfast napping."

"Alone?"

"Of *course*."

I smiled at her careless answer. "That *is* interesting because you don't have an alibi. But you do have a motive, don't you, Carla? You want everyone to believe that you and Greg are the perfect couple with a fairy tale marriage, but that's not the real story. And you had the opportunity to follow your friend to see what she was up to. I have to wonder if there isn't a lot more behind this girl's weekend than just old roommates getting together for fun."

Carla leaned right into my face, her breath hot and smelly. I leaned away from her.

"Let me tell *you* something," she said with a smirk like an evil stepmom. "Go ask Laura some questions. She plays the strong silent type, but that only hides her motives. You are right about one thing. This weekend was about more than a simple get-together. I wanted to know exactly what Greg and Ginger have been up to, and I think I got my answer. But, Laura's part of the picture too, and I haven't figured that out yet."

Carla stared at me for a couple more seconds before she turned and walked away with her head held high and her curls doing their dance.

Tilly handed me a thick strawberry smoothie. "Here, you look like you need something to wash her out of your system. I heard every word she said, and I can't decide if she killed Ginger because she was involved with her husband, or if she's about to kill her husband because he was involved with Ginger."

I tasted the smoothie. "Delicious, but it doesn't taste like our normal strawberry smoothie."

Tilly grinned. "Glad you like it. Sunny, I thought you knew that I never follow a recipe. If you must know, I added some kiwi, honey, and a splash of fresh lemon juice. Don't ask me for amounts because I didn't write anything down. You can be sure that no two smoothies of mine will ever taste the same."

As long as she didn't make anything for paying customers, we might squeak by without any problems. That was probably too much to hope for, though.

I enjoyed every drop of the smoothie before my mind got back to Carla's insinuations. "Those four women," I said, "are hiding secrets, and we've only scratched the surface."

"What now?" Hitch asked.

"Find Greg. If he's innocent, he's not about to go down for something he didn't do."

"And if he's guilty?" Tilly asked.

"Good question," I said, since I had no answer.

First, we had to find him.

21

With Dani jumping in and helping make shakes and smoothies, I had a few minutes to check on the kittens in our jungle greenhouse. Of course, that was really my excuse to ask Violet and her friends some more questions. They'd never suspect anything. I hoped.

I walked past the customers ordering fruity shakes and over-the-top pastries, ignoring the intoxicating aroma of coffee and freshly baked donuts to push on with my mission. No time to eat the profits, Sunny, I told myself as I entered the garden area.

"Hi, ladies," I said with as much cheer as I could muster. Jasper and Pip rushed to greet me. Jasper with her thick tail fanning behind her and Pip jumping on my legs for attention. At least they were thrilled to see me but the three women? Not so much.

They clamped their mouths closed. The sudden silence was an obvious tell that they'd been talking about me, or the murder, or probably both.

"Quite a day!" I said as I plopped down in a chair, inviting myself into their circle. I picked up Clawdia and gave her a cuddle.

"Can you believe it?" I looked at each of the women. "Someone abandoned this cutie-patootie right out back. Chief Bullock found her in a basket. People," I said with disgust. "But now that she's cleaned up, fed, and happy, I'm sure I'll find a good home for her."

"That's terrible," Laura said, showing honest emotion for the first time. "Who would do a terrible thing like that?"

I was glad to discover that there was at least one animal lover in this small group. I already knew that Violet wasn't a big fan of animals or most people for that matter. And Carla only had time to worry about her husband. Thank you, Clawdia, for helping me break the ice.

"I wish I knew," I said handing the puff of fluff to Laura, "but at least they left her where she'll be well taken care of. I suppose that's all that matters."

Laura held the kitten up and looked into her golden eyes. "You're one lucky girl. What about these other kittens?" she asked, cuddling Clawdia in her lap. "Are they all up for adoption?"

"Yes. Didn't Violet explain that to you? She volunteered to help out today. Jasper here is the official Chief Kitty Nanny but unfortunately, she can't help people with the adoption applications." I gave Jasper a hearty pat on her side and turned toward Violet. "Did anyone fill out a form today?"

A blush of pink filled her cheeks. "No. A few people came in, but no one asked me anything about the kittens. We've been talking a lot," she added sheepishly.

In other words, she hadn't paid any attention to the kittens. I'd bet that talking was *all* they'd been doing. I made a quick head count to be sure none of the kittens had escaped; all were accounted for. Jasper had two curled up with her and Pip was trying to make friends with Mama Cat. Her other two kittens were curled up together in a spot of sunshine that had finally broken through the clouds.

"I've been wondering," I said trying to sound casual. "What did you do yesterday after you left here? You must have had your weekend packed with activities. Right? And there's so much to do around Blueberry Bay."

Violet, always the spokesperson for the group, slid forward in her chair. "We did have plans but with Ginger disappearing," she frowned, "our day turned into a mixed-up mess. I guess that's the best way to describe it."

"That's right," Carla piped in. "We decided to all go our separate ways, see the town, buy some souvenirs, that sort of thing."

"And then meet up back at my house for dinner," Violet added. "Where you and Tilly crashed our get-together, in case you forgot." Her snippy tone? Duly noted, but not my problem, Violet. Of course, I didn't say that, but smiled to encourage Laura's take on things.

"I arrived at Violet's house right on time, but Carla and Violet weren't even there yet," Laura said with a touch of disgust. "I'm the only one, besides Ginger, who could be counted on to be where I said I'd be at the appointed time. I don't know why it's so hard for you two to plan better. It's rude, you know."

Good old, Laura, the downer in the group.

"Well," Violet huffed indignantly. "I had to get the wine. It wasn't my fault that there was a line at the store. I expected to zip in and out, but it took me longer than I expected."

Laura had been studying her nails like they held more importance than her two boring friends. "Exactly my point. You need to plan in extra time for unexpected events."

"Like you planned in extra time for this unexpected murder, Laura? Give me a break." Carla fidgeted in her seat like she had sand in her panties. "Greg and I walked on the beach before he dropped me off for my nap. I guess I just overslept a bit, but how can you blame me after all the worry about Ginger?"

"Where did Greg go?" I asked before someone changed the subject.

"Yes, Carla," Laura said with a smirk on her face. "Where *did* Greg go? You usually have his every second planned and supervised. Don't tell me you actually gave him time off for good behavior?"

And just like that, the air around this cozy get-together crackled with electricity.

"Girls!" Violet stood up and glared at me. I must have gotten under her skin. "Enough of this sniping. We were all concerned about Ginger yesterday and what difference does it make what we did besides worry, worry, and worry some more. As a matter of fact, I drove around looking for her but that turned out to be futile."

She turned quickly and pointed at me. "What about you, Sunny? Here you are constantly interrupting our private conversations with your ridiculous questions. I know what you're up to and that's why I came here today. You thought I wanted to help. Ha! I'm keeping an eye on you and *your* friends. What were *you* all up to yesterday when poor Ginger was missing?"

I let the question hang in the air as I calmed myself with a deep breath of the lavender-scented greenhouse air. I stifled a chuckle at Violet's ridiculous question.

"I'm glad you asked, Violet, but I'm also surprised that you had to. Did you forget that yesterday was the grand opening of Shakes and Cakes? I mean, most of the town showed up to enjoy our offerings, which kept Hitch, Tilly, Conrad, Jasper, and myself busy working. All day. Right here. So, I'm not sure what the point of your question was unless you think I hid Ginger's body under one of these benches of flowers and moved her at the end of the day."

All three women looked at the bench I'd pointed to like they thought I'd been serious.

Violet pushed a pot with the toe of her shoe. I dove to save it before it tipped and cracked in two. How careless, I thought.

Violet snorted. "You're quick, I'll give you that. Your sarcastic comment about Ginger could have truth behind it. Maybe that's exactly what you did. No one saw her after she visited you and Hitch here. You sent Chief Bullock and Officer Walker around in circles trying to find her and then—poof—like magic, where did she turn up? Right in Hitch's kitchen. The person she'd been looking for. My goodness, Sunny. How do you explain that?"

Carla and Laura seemed to be enjoying our duel.

"For now," I said, "I think someone staying at the Bayside Bed and Breakfast followed Ginger. That's how I explain what happened to Ginger."

They all started laughing. But it wasn't one of those deep ha, ha, ha's. It was more the nervous type of laugh as they eyed each other. Apparently, I'd hit a nerve. Or three.

I held my hand up. "This isn't a joke. Greg admitted that he saw Ginger walking along the road, not far from where Hitch found her in his apartment. Maybe he followed her inside and killed her."

"Or you, Carla," I continued. "Napping? I find that hard to believe since you don't let Greg out of your sight. I think it's more likely that you saw Ginger after Greg dropped you off, and you were worried they had plans to meet up, so you followed her."

Her eyes flew open, but she didn't look at her friends as a thick silence fell around us. These three women, who'd been so flippant moments earlier, now sat on the edge of their seats, probably holding their breath wondering what I would say next.

"And you, Laura, always so quiet, and watchful of everyone else. You could have seen Greg leave and wondered what he was up to. You're the one who said he's always flirting. You can never have enough ammunition to use against your so-called friends."

Her cheeks colored to match the pink hibiscus flowering in one corner of the greenhouse.

"Violet. Don't think I'm leaving you out. Last, but not least." Her smirk vanished. "You just said you were driving around looking for Ginger. Maybe you found her and decided to get even for some long ago slight. I was told that Ginger held grudges forever. What did she have on each of you?" I punctuated that question with a finger pointing from Violet, to Laura, to Carla.

"So, if you want to know what I've been doing? The answer is looking for Ginger's killer. I don't like it that someone followed her into Hitch's apartment. I don't like that it could have been an attempt to frame him. But it didn't work. Because Hitch and I were working all day."

I stood up. "Enjoy your stay here in Pineville, girls."

I bent over so I was at eye level with them. "Did you all work together to get rid of Ginger? Or," I straightened, "are you wondering who the killer among your group is?"

I left the greenhouse.

I was positive that my speech would settle over those women like a noose.

Sooner or later, one of them would make a stupid move to reveal their crime.

22

I left the relative quiet of the greenhouse behind and entered the bustling, noisy shake shop. It felt like one extreme to another. In a good way.

Conrad met me at the door. "What happened in there?" he asked. "We're dying of curiosity."

Tilly, Dani, and Hitch joined our circle at the edge of the serving counter.

I glanced over my shoulder at the three women packing up their things. "Violet and her entourage will be leaving shortly. Not that they did anything while they were here."

Tilly rolled her eyes. "Typical Violet. I was suspicious as soon as I saw her at your door this morning."

"Was it something you said?" Hitch asked. I didn't miss the smirk on his face.

"No doubt about it," I said, letting a grin fill my face. I poured myself a glass of water and lowered my voice. "They didn't like that I accused them of killing their friend, Ginger. Imagine that."

Conrad snorted. "You didn't!"

"Yeah, I did. I even accused them of all working together." I angled myself to see the greenhouse reflected in the door. Sure enough, they had slung their purses over their shoulders like weapons and headed our way.

Conrad quickly moved to open the door. "Oh, excuse me ladies. Are you leaving?"

Their faces were a study in disgust with maybe a little worry mixed in. They stomped silently past us without looking left or right.

Tilly, being Tilly, *had* to have the last word. "Have a nice day, girls" she shouted to their backs just before they escaped outside. Not surprisingly, they ignored her. Then, with a perfectly straight face, she looked at me and said, "Such a miserable group, aren't they?"

I couldn't hold it in any longer. A deep belly laugh rumbled up from inside. It was contagious, since my companions all doubled over, too. Oh, my goodness. It felt so good to have a hearty laugh to release all the tension from the morning. And the day before.

Customers enjoying a donut and shake in the shop looked at us and laughed too. Not sure why, but who cared? Laughter was always a welcomed tonic.

Conrad was the first to get himself under control. Through one last snort, he said, "Now I can hang out with the kittens for a bit."

I moved behind the counter, but before I helped the next customer, I said, "Conrad, you've been a huge help around here. Are you sure you have the time?"

He rubbed his hands together, a big smile on his face. "I need my fur ball fix before I head off to a job. I'll just make a quick check and make sure Jasper has everything under control." Then he saluted and disappeared into the greenhouse.

When Hitch passed behind me, he gave my shoulder a squeeze sending delightful tingles down my arm. "Good job in there, Sunshine," he whispered in my ear creating more shivers. "From the looks on those ladies faces, I think you gave them plenty to worry about."

"That was my plan. Carla basically threw Greg

under the bus and the others are all looking at each other wondering who did what."

"So, who did kill Ginger?" he asked.

"I wish I knew the answer to *that* question," I said out of the side of my mouth as I took the order for a banana strawberry supreme shake.

"Oh, hi, Hitch," a syrupy voice said from the other side of the counter. "Fancy seeing you here."

I recognized that phony baby doll purr and looked up to see Ashley with her eyes glued to Hitch, flirting as if no one was looking. And, I hadn't warned him yet.

"Ashley?" Hitch said. "What can I do for you?"

She giggled. "Seriously, Hitch? I can think of plenty."

I pinched myself before I jumped over the counter and throttled her. And, in case she'd decided that I was invisible, I squeezed myself in front of Hitch and forced a smile.

"Good morning, Ashley," I said, taking charge of the situation. I gave Hitch a shove away from us and hoped he'd take the hint and make himself scarce. "Have you decided what you want to order?"

Her eyes narrowed into slits. "I was talking to Hitch."

I turned around and looked behind me. "Well,

he has other duties to take care of, so now you're talking to me." I leaned over the counter close to Ashley's face and dropped my friendly voice like a rock. "What are you doing here?"

She crossed her arms and tilted her chin. "I have information for Hitch. Not you. I'll be sitting at that table over there." She nodded her head toward a corner table. "Tell him, if he wants to know what I saw, he'd better find a minute to spare. Believe me, it'll be worth it."

I didn't believe her or trust her, but I did want to know what she had to say.

Tilly arrived at the counter and put in several orders from a party at the table by the window. "What's up with her? Didn't she do enough damage already by siccing Officer Walker on me? She was sitting in her car when I went into Hitch's house yesterday. She's definitely got some strange habits."

"You saw her?" I said. I stuck the orders in the queue. Business was heating up again, four orders ahead of these. "She told me you didn't." I needed to get busy making shakes and serving cakes, but I needed to hear Tilly's news.

"Of course, that's what she'd say, Sunny. I didn't wave or even look at her, but I saw her sitting in that old beater she has, tapping her fingernails on the steering wheel. If I didn't know better, I'd say she was waiting for someone."

That fit with what I knew about Ashley. "Probably Hitch. She told me she likes to accidentally on purpose bump into him."

Tilly shook her head. "Pathetic. Listen, she was parked in front of the apartment when I arrived, but when I left, her car was empty. I guess she'd finally gone inside. What's she doing here?"

I looked at her sitting at the table, tapping the heel of her foot on the floor. I wondered how long she'd wait. "She wants to talk to Hitch. She said she has something interesting to tell him."

An evil grin spread across Tilly's face. "I have something to tell *her*."

I reached across the counter to grab Tilly's arm but came up with a handful of air. She was halfway across the shop making a beeline to Ashley. I rushed over to Hitch. He'd had his back to us, restocking the pastry display. "Get over there before Tilly makes a scene. Ashley wants to talk to you. She says it will be worth your time."

"She's nothing but trouble." He wiped his hands on his apron and arrived at Ashley's table as quietly as a cheetah. Ashley and Tilly were going at it, their voices drowning out everything in the shop.

Ashley looked startled to see him and her eyes widened. "Hitch. You look angry."

"Let's go outside, Ashley." Not giving her a choice, he took her arm, but Tilly maneuvered her way between them and took over the task of pulling Ashley to the door.

Dani pushed me away from the shake area. "Get out there with him before she accuses one of them of harassment or something. I'll stay here."

I wiped my brow and followed the trio outside. The salty breeze dried the sweat on my forehead as I joined them.

"What's so important, Ashley?" Hitch asked. I could see the fire in his eyes and some fear in Ashley's.

"I only want to help," she whimpered. "That guy's been sitting in his car outside our apartment building for at least an hour. Maybe longer."

"What guy?"

"The same guy I saw yesterday."

I jumped in and fired questions at her. "What does he look like? What kind of car?"

"A sporty car. Dark. He was slouched down in the seat so I couldn't really see him. He's been wearing sunglasses even though it's been mostly cloudy all day. He gave me the creeps."

Tears slid down her cheeks, and I almost felt sorry for her. Almost because I couldn't tell if this was an act, a lie, or something real. That's the problem when someone has already spun a tale to get someone else in trouble.

Ashley put her hand on Hitch's arm. "Please, I'm really worried. Especially," she glanced at me. "After *she* told me the killer might come after me if he knows I heard something through the wall that separates our kitchens."

Tilly pulled me away from Ashley's tear-filled story.

"Do you remember seeing a dark sports car when we left Violet's house last night?"

I closed my eyes, letting the scene replay in my memory. Tilly and I had walked away from Carla, Laura, and Greg, passing Officer Walker. I recalled Chief Bullock standing with Violet, ready to take her inside for questioning. I visualized Violet's path bordered by flower beds until we got to the street. It was quiet.

"Yes!" I said. "There was a dark sports car parked in front of Violet's house. It wasn't there when we first walked over. Do you think it was Greg's car?"

Tilly nodded. She pulled me toward her car. "Let's go."

23

"Wait!" I shouted and stopped. Tilly jerked backwards since our arms were linked together. "We have to tell Hitch what we're doing or he'll worry."

"There's no time," Tilly said and yanked hard on my wrist, trying to make me budge. "The guy in the car might drive away."

I unhooked myself from Tilly and said, "You go if you want. But I'm getting Hitch. Maybe we should call the police instead."

Tilly threw up her hands, clearly frustrated. "And tell them what? That there's someone sitting in his car on the side of the road? Officer Walker is already out to get me. Calling in some vague complaint will surely put me right back in his crosshairs."

"Okay," I said, heading back to the shop. "I get it. Just wait here for two seconds."

I jogged back to Hitch who was busy trying to calm Ashley down. As she blubbered on his shoulder, he patted her back and made some shushing noises. He looked over her head at me and rolled his eyes like he was stuck being her savior whether he liked it or not. I felt like throwing up.

Was Ashley putting on a helpless act to get Hitch's sympathy? Who knew? She'd already proven to be someone prone to exaggeration at best and an outright liar at the worst.

"Hitch?" I jerked my thumb to the side to let him know I needed to talk to him. In private.

He held Ashley at arm's length and forced her to look at him. "Ashley. Go inside. Tell Dani to fix you a mint chocolate chip milkshake. My treat. Then, sit down at one of the tables and pull yourself together. I'll be in when I'm done out here. Okay?"

She nodded and swiped the tears off her cheeks with the back of her hand, leaving big, dark streaks of mascara under her eyes. Not a look she'd like but I wasn't going to say anything to her.

"You two have something cooked up?" Hitch said

once Ashley had disappeared inside our shop. He didn't sound happy about it either. "Does it have something to do with the dark sports car Ashley told us about?"

"Who's driving?" Tilly yelled at us as she dug in her bag for her keys, which more or less answered her own question. "Hitch, Sunny and I both remember seeing a dark sports car in front of Violet's house last night. We think it belongs to Greg, so let's get a move on before he vanishes."

She was already behind the steering wheel of her bug and had the engine revving. There was no slowing Tilly down when she had her eye on the prize. Or suspect, in this case.

Hitch held my arm, catching me with one foot in Tilly's car. "One of us has to stay here. We do have a business to run." He ran his fingers through his hair, making it stick out in all directions. "I see Tilly won't be stopped, but please don't do anything foolish. Just drive by the car and get the license plate number. Under no circumstances should you try to talk to the person. Understand? He could be dangerous. I'll stay here to keep an eye on Ashley. I'm not sure what her game is."

"Thankfully, Dani stepped right in and has been super helpful," I said. "I can't say I'd choose to spend my day off volunteering at someone else's business, but I'll take it. We'll owe her big time after today."

"Yeah. Maybe a kitten?" He grinned at me, and I couldn't help but smile back. He had that way about him to know how to ease even a bad situation.

"Let Sunny go, Hitch, or she might lose a leg."

To prove her point, Tilly revved the engine again. I felt the vibration in the sole of my foot that rested on the mat in front of the passenger seat. The problem was that the rest of me was still outside the car. If Tilly got any more impatient, I'd likely lose more than my leg, which was *not* a pleasant thought.

Hitch gave me one last squeeze for good luck and let go. I plopped onto the seat in the bug, and Tilly started backing out before I'd slammed my door closed.

"Geez, Tilly. You're going to kill us both if you don't slow down."

"Close your eyes if you don't like my driving. I'm not slowing down."

I pulled my seat belt extra tight and gripped the edges of the seat. How many times had I told myself not to ride with this maniac? Too many, but here I was.

"Watch out!" I screamed as she drove over the dividing line.

Tilly laughed and swerved back into her lane. "Oops! I got a little distracted."

"If you aren't careful, Officer Walker will pull you over. How many warnings do you already have?" I knew this wasn't really playing fair but scaring her a little was my strategy to arrive in one piece.

The car immediately slowed to a reasonable speed. One that was barely over the thirty-five-mile per hour speed limit in this residential area. My survival increased by a hundred percent. I let out a big sigh of relief.

"You really know how to be a killjoy, Sunny." Tilly rocked the steering wheel back and forth making the bug do a little dance. But at least she stayed in her lane.

"Just looking out for your future, Tilly," I said. And mine I added silently.

She turned onto Hitch's street. "Here we are. Do you see that dark sports car?"

Tilly inched along at barely five miles an hour now. She could control herself when she needed to.

"There!" I saw what we were looking for about a quarter mile ahead. "That's it, parked opposite Hitch's apartment. Just drive by slowly, and I'll jot down the license plate number. I promised Hitch we wouldn't stop."

"*I* never promised him I'd do a simple drive-by, Sunny. Didn't you know that it's a lot more fun to break some rules?" And so much more dangerous. Instead of passing the car in question, Tilly stopped right behind it.

My heart rate jumped at least twenty beats a minute higher. Knowing Tilly, I should have seen this action coming, but if I acted quickly, I could keep her in the car. But as I jotted down the out of state plate number, Tilly opened her door.

"What are you doing?"

"What? You think I drove over here to sit and twiddle my thumbs? I want to talk to this guy and find out what he's up to."

Before I could stop her, she slid out of the car. I reached for her arm, but with the seat belt still tight across my chest, I came up short and Tilly slipped out of my grasp.

"He could be dangerous," I said.

Tilly hiked up her skirt to reveal a thigh holster. "Come on, Sunny. Do you really think that I'd jump into an adventure unprepared for the unexpected?"

Yes, as a matter of fact, that was a distinct possibility in Tilly's world.

"Never!" she said with a pleased chuckle. She closed the door and approached the driver's door.

I fumbled with my seat belt determined to join her. If nothing else, two against one made for better odds. I hoped I was right.

I watched as Tilly leaned down to look through the driver's window. She squinted, moved closer with her face practically squished against the glass.

Something was wrong inside Greg's flashy sports car.

24

My stomach twisted into a knot when I saw Tilly cup her hands around her face and peer through the sports car's window.

"What are you looking at?" I whispered, not sure I wanted to hear her answer.

"I'm not sure. Do you think he's dead?" She tapped her fingernails on the window... click, click, click.

Dead? This couldn't be happening.

I pushed her away and looked for myself. It was definitely Greg inside, slumped forward with his chin resting on his chest. At least I didn't see any blood oozing from any wounds. He had his phone clutched in his hand. I pulled on the door handle.

Locked.

I slammed my palm against the window and shouted, "Greg! Are you okay?" I knew my voice wouldn't bring him back if he *was* dead but I hoped it would wake him if he was asleep.

"Get out of the way, Sunny," Tilly ordered. "I'll *shoot* that door open."

She stood a couple of feet away from me, her legs set apart, and with both hands she gripped her pistol and pointed it at the car door.

I leaped forward before she pulled the trigger. "No! Put that thing away. You might hit him." Or me. I turned back to the window and pounded on it some more. Please, please, please, open your eyes. Do *something*.

The next thing I knew, Tilly had the passenger door open. Okay, I had to admit she was thinking much more clearly than I was in this bizarre situation. She reached across the passenger seat and gave Greg's shoulder a hard shake.

Finally, thank goodness, he lifted his head and blinked. "What? Where am I? What's going on?" he mumbled and wiped some drool off his chin.

My body crumpled against the car. I could barely stay upright after the shock of seeing him come back to life, but I managed to knock on his window and point to the buttons. "Unlock. Your. Door," I said slowly and clearly.

He didn't move.

Tilly reached over Greg and hit the unlock button so I could pull the door open.

The odor of alcohol practically overpowered me. That explained a lot about Greg's situation.

I coughed and breathed through my mouth to avoid a cloud of whatever rotgut had put him in this condition. "What are you doing here?" From his wrinkled shirt, disheveled hair, and empty bottle of cheap whiskey on the floor, he looked like someone who'd given up on caring about much of anything.

Greg stared at me, or more accurately, he stared right through me.

Tilly gave his shoulder another good shake. "Greg. Get out of this car right now. You're coming with us."

"What?" I squeaked. "That's not necessary." What I really wanted to say was, now that we know he's not dead, we don't want anything to do with him in case he's the killer.

"You're coming to my house for a strong cup of coffee. If you behave, I might even share my mint chocolate chip ice cream with you. That fixes everything." She gave him a push. Instinctively, I caught him before he crashed face first onto the curb.

"Help me over here, Tilly. He's more unmanageable than a sack of potatoes."

"Just don't take me back to Carla and her friends," he mumbled while I struggled to get him out of the car and onto his feet. "I can't deal with them anymore. I only came along this weekend so I could be with Ginger and now..."

I gripped him under one armpit, and Tilly supported his other side as we pulled, and he stumbled along with us to her bug.

"And now she's gone." He blubbered like a two-year-old who'd skinned his knee.

We shoved him in the back of Tilly's bug, head-first, where he collapsed in a heap. I gulped in air after the exertion of moving almost two hundred pounds of dead weight. Then I looked at her over the roof of her car. "What now?"

"Coffee. Didn't you hear me half a minute ago? We need to sober him up and pick his brain about Ginger."

"Are you sure that's a good idea? We don't know anything about this guy."

"Exactly."

When Tilly rolled her eyes, I knew she'd lost her patience with me.

"Now get in," she said in her stern, no-nonsense voice. "This is our chance to find out everything he knows. This guy probably has all the scoop on those roommates' secrets. Or, do you want to wait for our friendly Officer Walker to drum up something else against me and haul me back to the police station? You know he has it in for me one way or another."

I looked at Greg, slouched on the back seat with his eyes closed over a tear-streaked face. A loud snort erupted. At the moment, he did look fairly harmless.

"Okay," I said after I'd slipped onto the front seat. "I hope he doesn't throw up in your brand spanking new car, though."

"He'd better not or I'll shoot him." She patted her leg. Her pistol made a slight bulge under her skirt as a reminder.

"That's a great idea, Tilly. You know what?" I looked at her with my best serious face. "That way you'll turn the inside of your car into the same nice red color as the outside AND give Officer Walker a *real* reason to lock you up."

She looked at me. A grin spread across her face. "You finally found your sense of humor. I think now we're ready for phase two of this secret undercover operation."

I shook my head. It was no use trying to talk any sense into Tilly. She loved drama, and right now she was in her element.

"Okay. I'm all ears," I said, knowing it was much better to hear her plan than be surprised by whatever was marinating in her brain.

"Well, I just thought of a slight adjustment. We'll go to *your* house in case the suspects, you know who I mean, are next door. We might be able to eavesdrop on them through your fence."

Before I digested this, a strong hand, reaching from behind my seat, gripped my shoulder.

I never knew my lungs could emit such a blood curdling scream. Actually, I realized that it was both Tilly and me screaming. This big distraction made Tilly take her eye off the road and her little Volkswagen bug swerved left and right and then headed straight toward a maple tree at the side of the road.

I screamed louder, not knowing that was possible either.

I looked at Greg, his hand on my shoulder and

now sitting up in the back seat with his wide eyes focused on the tree coming toward us.

Tilly came to her senses, sort of, and slammed her foot on the brake. She forgot about the clutch and the bug jerked to a sudden stop, sending Greg forward, crashing into the back of my seat with a bone-crunching thud.

I patted my chest, thankful for my seatbelt.

At least Greg had his hands to himself now, instead of on our shoulders. He clutched his face as blood dripped through his fingers. Well, it was more than a drip and it was making a mess in the back of Tilly's car.

"You shouldn't have a license!" he yelled at Tilly. "Are you trying to kill us?"

He was the second person in two days to tell Tilly she shouldn't have a license, and I was sure that she wouldn't listen to either of them.

"Kill *you* maybe but not us. We're wearing our seat belts which saved us when my lightning reflexes hit the brake stopping us just in the nick of time from crashing into that tree."

Now that I knew I was, in fact, still alive and, more importantly, unhurt, I let myself look out the windshield. The stately maple tree, only inches from the front bumper, hadn't flinched at Tilly's close call. Of course not, I told myself, it's a tree.

"Here." Tilly threw a handkerchief to Greg. "Clean yourself up and stop dripping blood in my car." She backed up and headed toward my house.

She was back on track with her plan.

I shuddered at the thought.

25

Tilly zipped into my driveway.

Greg groaned in the back seat but hadn't tried to strangle me or otherwise cause a problem, so I relaxed a little. Maybe he was afraid of Tilly. Or, maybe he wasn't the bad guy. Time would tell.

"How's your nose, Greg? Did the bleeding stop?" Tilly asked, sounding slightly sympathetic.

"Broken, I'm sure."

"Come on inside. Sunny will get some ice for you. I've got to run over to my house for a minute."

"Huh? You're leaving me alone with him? I don't even have Jasper to help." Forget about that five seconds of relaxing I'd just enjoyed.

"Take this, then." Tilly reached under her skirt and tried to hand me her pistol.

Greg fell back against the seat. "I'm not going inside. At least out here, someone might hear me scream for help or see you shoot me so you don't get away with murder."

Like you? I almost said but I didn't want to play that card yet. Instead, I shook my head and refused the gun. Greg wasn't paying attention so maybe I could bluff my way to staying alive.

Tilly pushed her seat forward and pulled on his arm. "Greg, no one's going to shoot you if you don't do anything stupid. Follow Sunny, she's much nicer than I am."

Normally, I would have appreciated that compliment, but under these circumstances I'd rather have Greg think I was mean and nasty. And maybe even trigger happy.

"Besides," Tilly said, "If you stay out here you might get a visit from Violet, or one of the other *girls*, including your wife. Their cars are all parked next door. Is that what you prefer? I could arrange it very easily. I have Violet's number on speed dial." She even held up her phone.

I knew that was a lie. I doubted Tilly had ever

called Violet in her life, but Greg didn't need to know that detail. He was stuck between me or three women he was trying to avoid like the plague. Especially his wife. It didn't sound like a difficult choice to me.

"Okay. I'll go with Sunny. She's by far the best option."

Tilly flashed me a thumbs up before she jogged across the street. Tilly's demolition derby demonstration shook Greg out from some of his alcoholic haze, enough for him to pour himself out of the back of her bug without my assistance, though he had to lean on my shoulder to navigate my front walk into my house. Princess Muffin and Stash jumped off the couch and stalked us as soon as I closed the door. A bit of normalcy in this upside-down day.

"You have kittens here, too?" Somehow, somewhat unsteadily, Greg crouched down and scooped them both into his arms. The kittens gave him affectionate head butts which actually made him smile. He plopped onto the floor and talked to them as if they were babies. Could a man who unabashedly cooed to kittens be a killer?

"Stay where you are, Greg. I'll be right back."

I'm not sure he heard me; the kittens had his full attention. I got some ice from my freezer and wrapped it in a towel for his rapidly swelling nose.

"Yes," I said when I returned. "There never seems to be a shortage of kittens needing good homes. Are you a cat person?" I asked even though answer was crawling over his arms and heading for his neck. "Can you put Princess Muffin down for a few minutes and sit on the couch while I take care of your injury?"

He shed himself of my menagerie and said, "I love cats, but *Carla*," he rolled his eyes, "says she's allergic. I wish she was allergic to *me*."

Here was the perfect opening. "So, tell me, Greg," I said as I tilted his head back and arranged the ice pack on the bridge of his nose. "What's the deal with the roommates? I didn't get the feeling that they are actually fond of each other."

I give him credit. He was a good patient. I took his hand and placed it on the ice pack to hold it in place. "Ha!" he said around the bulky device. "You're very perceptive. You picked up on their dysfunctional relationships quickly. I'm sort of used to it after all these years."

"Oh?" I raised my eyebrows hoping he'd spill the dirt.

My door opened, spoiling the moment.

Tilly entered juggling her coffee carafe and a tub of ice cream. "Have I got news for you two," she said enthusiastically after she'd kicked the door closed. "But first, mint chocolate chip ice cream," which she set on my coffee table like it was a bigger present than winning the lottery. Well, with Tilly's addiction, that might be true.

"And coffee," she added with a nod toward Greg. "Then I'll tell you what I just saw." She grinned at us and left us hanging on that comment as she rustled around in my kitchen for mugs, bowls, and spoons. I could have offered to help but decided to keep an eye on Greg in case he decided to make a run for it.

Returning with her loot, Tilly got right down to business scooping out huge portions for each of us while I poured the coffee.

"Dig in," she said.

Greg ignored his bowl of ice cream but managed to sip his coffee while holding the ice on his nose. "Jealousy. To answer your question, Sunny, the roommates are all jealous of each other. Or, maybe envy is more accurate. One makes more money than everyone else. One is prettier. Another one is smarter. I've tried to stay out of all the drama, but Carla always wants me to choose sides, hers of course, which is an impossible position to be in."

He let out a long exhale, like he was glad *that* was

finally off his chest. He put down the ice and swapped it for the ice cream.

Both envy and jealousy were dangerous emotions. I could imagine that it might eat away over years and years until something happened to make someone snap. And that might lead a person to justify murder; that someone *deserved* to die. I shuddered at that thought but understood it could happen in a worst-case scenario.

I glanced at Tilly and raised my eyebrows. I couldn't help wondering what *she* thought of Greg's comments. She shrugged.

"Anyway," she said, scraping her bowl of every last bit of ice cream. "Laura just stormed out of Violet's house and drove away like a bat out of, you know where. Violet and Carla stood in the doorway looking like they'd just swallowed a week-old bowl of clam chowder. Kind of green around the gills if you know what I mean." She sat back and crossed her legs. "What do you think that could be about?" She looked at Greg.

"Interesting," he said. "It looks like they're choosing sides."

"I wonder if it had anything to do with our conversation at the Kitty Castle," I said, knowing I'd zapped a few nerves. "Violet and Carla against Laura?"

"Must have been quite the conversation," Greg said, finally giving me his full attention.

"Oh," I waved my hand dismissively. "Not that big of a deal unless one of them was hiding a big secret. I just put some ideas together, which led me to kind of sort of accuse each one of having a motive for murdering Ginger. And, much to my surprise, it didn't go over very well. You have to wonder whose secret had something to do with Ginger."

Greg's mouth dropped open. "I wish I'd been a fly on *that* wall."

"Or, one of the kittens," I said. "I also learned that Laura likes cats but Violet and Carla don't. And I really don't trust people that don't like animals."

Greg grinned at that last comment. "So, you trust *me*?"

"I wouldn't go as far as to say that yet." I didn't want him to get *too* comfortable. I felt my phone vibrate, which reminded me that I should really be at Shakes and Cakes helping Hitch instead of running around with gun-toting Tilly.

I checked the text message from Hitch: *Where are you? Everything okay?*

On our way back, I responded.

"Tilly, we gotta go. Right now. Hitch is worried."

"Drop me off at my car?" Greg asked. "I'm okay to drive thanks to your intervention." He gently massaged his nose. "This will be my reminder to watch out for a pistol packing lady driving a red Volkswagen beetle in the future."

"Nope," Tilly said as she headed to the door. "You're on our team now, Greg. You're staying with us."

What did she think this was, a baseball game?

Greg didn't move to follow us. "Come on," I said, frustration beginning to overwhelm me.

He held his hands out to the sides. "Can't move," he said with a what-do-you-want-me-to-do-about-this-problem expression.

"Oh." Stash and Princess Muffin were curled together on his lap, fast asleep and completely comfortable.

I gently lifted them off Greg's lap and placed them on the couch in a patch of sunshine where they usually liked to sleep.

It was hard to think of Greg as a potential murderer when he had such a soft spot for my kittens.

I hoped I wasn't letting my guard down too soon.

26

"Your team?" Greg shook his head once he was settled in the back seat again.

I knew how that sounded. To the inexperienced, dealing with Tilly was like falling into some kind of twilight zone with no exit. Don't get me wrong. I loved Tilly, but it had taken time to unlock her heart and understand the goodness behind her somewhat unconventional tendencies.

Greg was in for a bumpy ride if he chose to stick around.

"So," Tilly said, looking at Greg in the rearview mirror. At least she hadn't turned completely around. I kept my eye on the road in case I had to commandeer the steering wheel.

"Who do you think killed Ginger?" she asked. Assuming, of course, that it wasn't you."

Oh, did I mention blunt? Tilly liked to cut right to the heart of the matter.

Greg leaned between the two front seats and sputtered. "Is that what this... this *abduction* is all about? You think *I* killed Ginger?" He crashed back, smacking loudly against the seat.

Tilly looked at me.

"Watch out!"

"Oops." She'd wandered into the other lane but made a quick correction. "No harm done."

"I didn't say that, Greg," Tilly said in a soothing tone. "Why did you jump to that conclusion? You don't have a guilty conscience, do you?"

He folded his arms over his chest and looked out the side window. Tilly drove in silence, which meant she had something up her sleeve.

"I loved Ginger," Greg said eventually. His voice was so quiet I wasn't sure I'd heard him correctly.

"You what?" I asked.

"I loved her. It really wasn't much of a secret with the roommates. I had my eye on Ginger before I even met Carla. Ginger made it clear that she had other plans, of course. Carla tried to spin our marriage like it was this fairy tale romance right from the get-go. The truth was the complete opposite." He let his head fall back against the seat.

Now I understood Tilly's silence. She was giving Greg enough rope to hang himself, or at least time to get him talking.

"Let me guess," I said. "Laura strikes me as the one in the group who likes to stir up trouble, get under people's skin, especially needling Carla. Laura wasn't surprised at all when Tilly suggested that you and Ginger went off on a sightseeing trip together to explain Ginger's disappearing act."

"I already told you that I saw Ginger walking when I was on my way to Misty Harbor," he said. "What I didn't say is that I *did* stop to talk to her. All I wanted was to have a friendly conversation because she'd been avoiding me. I didn't know why. I'd long ago given up the idea that she and I could have anything beyond a friendship. Not because she was loyal to Carla. She couldn't care less about hurting anyone. No, she told me that she had her eyes on someone."

"Who?" I blurted out.

"I don't know, and I don't care." He sniffled, suggesting he cared. A lot. "She wouldn't say, except it was someone she'd met in New York. She wanted to get to know him better and was heading to his apartment."

Hitch? He'd met Ginger in New York. She'd left him multiple messages and texts. She'd found her way to his apartment and got herself murdered there. Tingles of fear crept up my spine. Was Greg spinning us a tale of woe to cover up his crime?

Tilly rubbed my arm. "I know what you're thinking. We'll get to the bottom of this. Sooner or later."

Tilly was right, and I was more determined than ever to find out what made Ginger go into Hitch's apartment and who followed her.

Greg's next words sliced right through me. "She did let me give her a ride, though. I don't think she realized how far it was when she decided to walk. That's how I know where the guy lives.

"Do the police know you gave her a ride?" I asked, trying to keep my voice calm.

"Of course, they don't. I'd be a fool to tell them something like that. Especially with Carla ready to throw me under the bus because of her jealousy. It worries me a little though. How did you two know where to find me today?"

I looked at him in the mirror of my visor, "Someone saw you sitting there in your car and thought it was kind of creepy." As annoying as

Ashley was, I wasn't going to identify her and risk Greg targeting her if he was more than an innocent bystander.

He stared out the window for a minute before his face lit up with a new revelation. "Must have been that blonde. She stared at me while I was drowning my sorrows before she scurried into her car. What's wrong with sitting in my car and minding my own business?"

So much for protecting Ashley. "It's creepy, Greg. This is a small town. People don't just sit in their car on the side of the road."

"Whatever. I wanted to get a look at the guy Ginger planned to meet."

My heart skipped a beat.

"Greg," Tilly said as she pulled into the Shakes and Cakes parking lot. "You never told us who *you* think killed Ginger."

I silently thanked Tilly for changing the focus away from Hitch.

"Here's the thing," he said. "Any one of the roommates could have done it. Carla hated Ginger. She was always jealous of her probably because she knew that Ginger was my first choice. With Ginger gone, maybe she thought I'd somehow miraculously fall in love with her the way I did with Ginger."

That made a lot of sense.

"But Laura had her reasons, too."

Oh boy.

"Laura was the smart, studious one in the group. She'd tutored Ginger through college, but then Ginger applied for the dream job that Laura expected to get after graduation, and guess what? Ginger got hired. Laura never forgave her."

"And, Violet?"

"Ah, yes, Violet. She worked for a few years before she went to college. She was older than the others. Always pinching pennies. She wanted to fit in with the group. Even when she didn't have the money to go to whatever restaurant or fun activity they'd all planned, Ginger would say, 'Oh come on, I'll treat'."

"Let me guess," I said. "Ginger didn't follow through with the money." I was starting to get a better picture of these so-called friends.

"Exactly," Greg said, slapping his knee for emphasis. "Violet graduated with a ton of debt from student loans and several maxed out credit cards that she blamed on Ginger."

Before we got out of the car, there was one more question I had to ask.

"Why did they come for this reunion if they didn't like each other?"

"Because it was Ginger's idea. They all wanted her to like them. It was another one of their competitions they never outgrew. Who did Ginger favor on any particular day? It was exhausting, and I didn't want to be part of it, but Carla insisted." He shrugged. "I figured I'd get to see Ginger, so I came along."

"What a mistake that turned out to be," I said.

But, was it? I wondered.

27

I slid off the passenger seat, anxious to find Hitch inside Shakes and Cakes. With day two of our new business almost over, I needed to know how we'd fared while I'd been out gallivanting with Tilly looking for a possible murder suspect.

Tilly waited for Greg to squeeze out of the back of her car. I was happy to leave her to babysit the passenger.

I inhaled deeply as I walked into the shop, savoring the aroma of the flowers scenting the air. The smiling customers and buzz of conversations sent a thrill of delight to my brain. Yes, our fledgling business was off to a great start.

Dani was busy behind the counter making

shakes while Hitch balanced a tray of drinks for several tables of Pineville locals. It was soothing to be back in my normal world instead of mired in Tilly's drama-filled adventure.

"Hey, handsome," I whispered as I sidled close to Hitch.

He spun around after delivering the last of the shakes to a recently-retired neighbor of mine, a grin filling his face. "Welcome back! I thought you'd decided you'd had enough of Shakes and Cakes and took off for a better adventure with Tilly never to be seen or heard from again."

I knew he was teasing, but I rolled my eyes as though he was serious instead of totally ridiculous. It was one of the things I liked about Hitch the most. He knew exactly what to say to help ease my tension.

"You can't even imagine what it's like to go off with her when she's on one of her missions," I said. "Walking in here is like returning to normal and a welcome dose of aroma therapy."

Hitch set two tall foamy strawberry shakes in front of Ruby Todd, the owner of A Donut A Day and her employee, Jessica Golden. "Here you go," he said. Are you sure I can't tempt you two lovely ladies with something from our delicious donut selection?"

Hitch had a twinkle in his eye and a special

charm that had the female customers always looking at him like they'd love to eat him up along with their shake and cake.

"Oh, come on, Hitch," Ruby said with a gentle pat on his arm. "We sample enough of our donuts while we're making them. Right, Jess?"

"Speak for yourself, hon, I limit myself to one a week and only when you create a new recipe."

Ruby talked to Hitch like they were accomplices. "Jess has so much self-control when it comes to eating. I have zero." Ruby laughed a loud deep belly laugh that filled the shop. "You only live once, I say, and I plan to enjoy this lifetime to the max. So, how's business been for you two?" She looked around the shop and nodded her approval at our renovations.

"We can't complain. It's been busy and we're getting positive feedback and return customers so, all in all, I'd say we're off to a fantastic start," Hitch said.

"And your donuts are a big hit, Ruby," I added. "I hope you'll keep supplying us."

"Are you kidding? It's the best thing that's happened to A Donut A Day in years. Some people might say it's a conflict of interest, but you know what I say?"

I shook my head wondering what piece of wisdom she planned to share next.

"Hogwash is what I say. We're all in this together and when someone tries a donut here, they stop for a dozen at my shop. Win-win, right?"

Hitch patted her shoulder. "I love your attitude."

Ruby pulled Hitch close. "We heard that murder victim stopped here yesterday morning before she disappeared. Did you know her?"

"I'd met her a couple of times, but I didn't know her at all. Hopefully," he glanced at me, "the police will wrap this up quickly."

"Oh, I know. It's just frightful to think there's a murderer on the loose in town, right, Jess? Especially with you doing all that dog walking and house sitting. I hope you're being extra careful."

"Walking dogs is probably the safest activity around. Who's going to mess with a barking four-legged bodyguard?"

Ruby snorted. "Your bodyguards are maybe twenty pounds when they're soaking wet. You really think they'll protect you?"

"You'd be surprised at how ferocious those small dogs are. As a matter of fact, Sunny, you have an adorable Jack Russel terrier in your greenhouse with Jasper and the kittens. Who's that?"

"You met Pip? She belongs to my friend, Dani Mackenzie from Misty Harbor. Dani owns the Little Dog Diner. They make the cupcakes that keep your donuts company in the pastry display. She made a delivery this morning and offered to stay and help since we were shorthanded."

"Well, there you go," Jess said as she looked at Ruby. "Pip proves my point that a powerhouse can come in a small package. I bet she can hold her own against just about anything."

I laughed at that image. "She can. So glad you two stopped by. Hitch and I had better get back to work before the help discovers they don't really need us."

Ruby laughed another one of her deep belly laughs. "I don't mind that at all. It gives me time off." She shook her finger at us. "Be sure to schedule some down time or you'll just burn yourselves out. That's my advice for today."

"Thanks Ruby."

"She's right, you know," I said to Hitch as we walked back to the counter. "We have to figure out how to balance work *and* our lives."

"It's only day two, Sunny. We have to get our routine perfected before we worry about taking time off. Speaking of which. You and Tilly were gone for a lot longer than I expected."

I glanced out the window where Tilly was still talking to Greg.

Hitch followed my gaze. "Don't tell me."

"Yeah, Tilly had a plan when we found the sports car and it didn't involve driving by and writing down the license plate number."

"I should have known," he said.

I filled him in on the important details we'd learned from Greg. "And now Tilly told Greg that he's on our team. I'm still not sure what that's supposed to mean. Hey," I jabbed Hitch with my elbow. "Ashley's still here?"

"She said she's not leaving until I do. She said she doesn't feel safe."

"It's just an excuse you know. She's obsessed with you," I said. Was I jealous?

"Listen. I can't stay at my apartment anyways with the police still searching for evidence. I told her she could follow me back to her apartment, and I'd make sure she got inside safely. Then I'll come to your place. Okay?"

"Well, I don't know." I couldn't keep a straight face. "Jasper might not be happy sharing the couch."

Hitch groaned. "Jasper snores. Maybe Tilly will put me up instead."

As we laughed at our silly banter, I kept my eyes on Ashley. "What's wrong with her? She just turned white as a ghost."

I looked outside to see what she was staring at. Tilly and Greg were still discussing something.

"Hitch, Ashley just saw Greg. She's probably afraid he'll come in here and see her. You'd better take her out through the greenhouse while I talk to Tilly and find out what her plans are for Greg."

I waited a few minutes for Hitch to convince Ashley to go with him, then I scooted outside. "Tilly, I need to talk to you."

She pointed to her car before she walked over to me.

"You have to get Greg out of here so Hitch can get Ashley home."

"I think I've convinced him to stay at my house. He was planning to sleep in his car, but I told him he'd probably get arrested."

"That's what you've been out here arguing about?"

"Pretty much. Let me know when you get home. Toodles!" She dashed over to her car, scarf flying behind her, and caught up to Greg. She probably didn't want to give him a chance to change his mind.

I wasn't sure that wouldn't be a good idea, but Tilly could hold her own against anyone.

I hoped.

28

Hitch got Ashley safely in her car, then found me in the shop. "I'll get her home and meet you back here."

"Perfect," I said, taking a sponge to a spill on the counter. "It's almost closing time so when you get back," I wiggled my eyebrows, "we can sit down for a few minutes to unwind." Before we have to find out what Tilly is up to, I said to myself. Hitch would find out soon enough that she'd invited Greg to stay at her house.

The last of our customers headed out of Shakes and Cakes with their arms filled with plants and to-go containers. I smiled and thanked them for stopping in.

Inside, Dani was busy wiping down the counter.

I didn't know how I'd ever thank her enough for staying and helping today, but I believed that someday I'd have the chance.

I slid onto a stool and made mental notes on her efficient system of closing up. "You saved us by jumping in and helping today, Dani. Thank you. I hope this type of problem doesn't become a daily event or we'll be out of business."

She paused with her cleaning rag. "I've learned one important thing from running the Little Dog Diner. Expect the unexpected. If you can pivot and make quick adjustments, you'll be fine. You and Hitch seem to have a good partnership, which is extremely important. And, everything does get easier with time."

"Boy, I hope so." I leaned on her cleaned counter with my cheek in my hand. "We brainstormed and thought we'd planned for every possibility, but who could have foreseen a murder throwing everything out of whack?" I looked at Dani and laughed. "Well, besides you," I added, thinking of all the disruptions in her life because of murders in Misty Harbor.

"Be careful. I know you were off with Tilly today, but asking questions and looking under rocks for clues can backfire."

"But—"

Dani held up her finger, silencing me. "I know what I'm talking about. Keep Jasper with you if you have to go someplace alone. I'm not foolish enough to think you won't try to get to the bottom of anything that impacts you or someone you love." She narrowed her eyes to drive home her point. "Just always *be careful*."

I nodded. What else could I do? She was right. I walked around the counter and hugged her. "Your friendship, your words of advice, everything," I blubbered through a few tears. "Thank you."

While we consoled each other and cemented our female friendship to a new level, at least in my opinion, I heard the greenhouse door open and close.

"Am I interrupting something?" Conrad asked as he and Pip entered the shop. His face told me he suspected the worst from our sobbing.

"Just some girl bonding. How are the kitties doing?" I asked, glad to change the subject to my magic fur balls.

"Lots of interest again today. But I'm afraid I have a lot of steep competition for Mama Cat once she can leave her babies. You know, if it helps to sweeten my chances, I'll adopt one of her kittens, too. Just so you know, it's my professional cat sitter opinion that Mama Cat likes me best anyway."

I laughed at his forlorn expression. "Don't worry, Conrad. Mama Cat can pick her new family and my guess is that will be you. We only have to wait a few more weeks."

Pip danced around Dani's legs, obviously excited to see her person. "Had fun today, Pipsqueak?" Dani picked her up and received a face wash for her trouble. She laughed and turned away from the busy tongue. "Okay, I guess that's a resounding *yes*."

After putting Pip down, Dani untied her apron and tried to scoop her tangle of auburn curls back into some kind of order before she grabbed her backpack. "We're heading home now, Sunny. Good luck with the problem that landed in your lap. I don't envy you."

I watched my good friend and her companion walk to her car just as Hitch drove in.

"I'm heading home now, too," Conrad said. "See you tomorrow?"

"Boy, I hope so. You can help Jasper whenever you want to."

"I have to stop in to say hello to Mama Cat, but I won't be able to stay all day. Unfortunately, I have some jobs to get back to."

"Thanks, Conrad. We'll be fine."

I opened the greenhouse door, needing a dose of Jasper's special soothing mellowness.

"Hey, girl. How was your day?"

Jasper carefully stepped around the kittens who'd been using her tail as some sort of jump rope. She greeted me with what almost looked like a smile, so I plopped onto one of the metal chairs. With her head resting on my lap, she let me know that she was ready for an ear massage.

"That's the spot?" She tilted her big head so I had easier access.

The greenhouse door opened and closed with barely a click to disturb the peaceful silence under the canopy of vines and orchid blooms.

Hitch pulled over a chair and sat next to me. "Ashley's home. She asked me to stay, but I managed to convince her to just lock her door and stay inside. The police were still searching my apartment so she shouldn't have anything to worry about."

I took that in, satisfied that Ashley's flirting with Hitch was getting her nowhere, so I changed the subject. "You know, this is my new favorite time of day. Everyone is gone except us, Jasper, and the kittens. This quiet in the greenhouse is just what I need right now. The flowers add a refreshing earthy aroma to the unique peacefulness in here. I love it, Hitch."

He took my free hand in his and squeezed. "That's music to my ears, Sunshine. We've created something special, but I wasn't sure you'd love the greenhouse part as much as I do."

"And all the customers that have stopped in. We'll need to hire more help soon if we hope to ever have time off."

We enjoyed the silence for several more minutes, but I knew it couldn't last forever. "Hitch?"

"Uh-huh," he answered in a dreamy tone.

"Tilly invited Greg to stay at her house. She wants me to let her know when I get home."

His eyes flew open. "What? He's the one who scared Ashley to death and now Tilly's babysitting him?"

"She's probably thinking it's better to keep him close where we can keep eyes on him instead of having him on the loose and possibly causing trouble. He told us that he gave Ginger a ride to your apartment. That's why he was sitting there. He wanted to check out this friend of hers."

"And that's supposed to make me feel better? What if Greg is Ginger's stalker? The guy she thought was out to hurt her?"

"I don't know, Hitch. I'm just telling you what Tilly's doing. You know as well as I do that she doesn't listen to anyone once she's made up her mind. Let's go to my house and find out what she has in mind for the next part of her plan." If she even *has* a plan, I added silently.

"I'm hungry," Hitch said. "That's the next part of *my* plan."

"Oh, I almost forgot. Dani left a surprise casserole in the fridge for us. The note said she knew we wouldn't feel like cooking. I'll grab it on the way out."

Hitch held his hand out and pulled me to my feet. "Sorry for sounding angry. It's been a long day. I can't go home, Ashley is a high maintenance neighbor, and now we have to deal with Greg. But," he smiled at me. His eyes tired but that familiar twinkle was still there. "I get to spend my time with you so there is a light at the end of my day."

I returned Hitch's smile but a twinge of dread about what might come next hung under the happiness.

29

A comfortable quiet filled Hitch's car as we drove to my house. Jasper, alert in the back, watched the scenery speed by. My loyal companion, always ready for anything.

Dani's casserole rested on my lap. Curiosity gnawed at me. Impatience won. I lifted a corner of the foil and peeked at the contents.

"Oh, Hitch, you won't believe what Dani made for us," I said, practically drooling at the sight of this treat. Thinking about food was a welcome distraction from trying to figure out why Ginger was murdered in his apartment. "Take a guess."

"Lasagna," he said without even thinking.

"Nope. Try again."

"Macaroni and cheese."

"You get half a point for that."

His face lit up. "*Lobster* mac and cheese?"

I pulled the foil back so Hitch could see the big chucks of pink lobster meat mixed in the macaroni under a crispy breadcrumb topping.

He licked his lips. "Well, my day is complete," he said, smiling broadly. "How'd she know that's what I've been craving for weeks?"

"Because we live on Blueberry Bay and it's pretty much everyone's favorite comfort food in all of Maine? Or, it's a lucky guess. Does it matter?"

He shook his head. "Not at all." He reached over and tried to grab a chunk of lobster, but I slapped his hand.

"That's disgusting. You have to wait. I'll make a salad and I have a bottle of chardonnay that I've been saving for a special occasion." Special occasion being pretty much any event that involved food and Hitch. "How does that sound?" I envisioned a relaxing evening, *not* filled with drama.

"Maybe we can sneak in, lock the door, and forget about Tilly. Enjoy this special gift, a glass of wine, and just relax," Hitch said like he'd read my mind.

"Maybe," I answered without much conviction. "She does have a key to my house, though. Unfortunately, there's no way to keep her out. And," I added, "we have to get this Ginger mess out of our lives before Officer Walker makes more trouble for us. I hate having it hang over our heads."

That thought dragged me down a notch and I stared at our quaint little town out my side window as Hitch drove us back to my place. Then Hitch broke into my solitude.

"You're right, Sunshine," he said, startling me with an unusually loud voice."

"Well, of course, I am." I chuckled. "But about what exactly?" I'd lost thread of our conversation.

"We have to figure out why Ginger decided to come to Pineville. Do you think the reunion was a cover for something else?"

He turned a corner and I grabbed our dinner before it went sideways off my lap. "Easy on the turns. We have a delicate load here."

Hitch laughed and I said, serious now, "That's a good question. According to Greg, if he can be believed, there was a lot of jealousy between the roommates. Ginger organized the reunion, even paid for the rooms at the Bayside Bed and Breakfast but never checked in or arrived at Violet's house when she'd promised. It's strange."

"Here's the thing, Hitch," I continued after more thoughts flooded my brain. "If Ginger really was worried about a stalker, *and* if she thought it was one of the roommates, she could have planned the reunion to get them all together in one place. She wanted to ask you to protect her, and it sounds like she was the type of person who was used to getting what she wanted. In her mind, it might have been a good plan to flush out her stalker and get that problem out of her life."

Hitch nodded and shot me a smile. "That makes about as much sense as anything else. What did she do from the time she left Shakes and Cakes yesterday morning and when she showed up at my apartment? Dead, don't forget."

Like I could forget a detail like that. "We might never know. You blew her off, so if she was truly scared, she might have just gone into hiding until she decided to go to your apartment and wait for you. She *did* end up in your apartment. Why else would she have gone there unless she felt desperate and confident she could convince you to help her?"

"That all sounds logical, Sunny, but why did she

leave her SUV at the bed and breakfast and walk? That just put her out in the open for her stalker."

"Yeah." I shrugged, knowing it was hopeless to try to figure out someone else's thought process, but I tried anyway. "Maybe she thought leaving her car was a decoy. I bet she had a suspicion about which roommate was after her."

I slapped my forehead. "That's it, Hitch!" I couldn't believe I hadn't thought of this before. "Ginger planned the reunion here in Pineville. Who lives here? Violet. Who called the police to report Ginger missing? Violet. Who was not staying at the bed and breakfast? Violet."

"I think I see a pattern in your thoughts, Sunshine." He grinned at me.

"That obvious?"

"Totally. But, it does all fit together in a too obvious way."

"Violet also let it slip that she was out buying wine and got delayed when the others arrived at her house last night. Maybe she was delayed because she saw Ginger and followed her to your apartment, killed her, and then rushed back to her house with her lame excuse."

Hitch pulled into my driveway and turned to face me, his face serious. "Are you sure you aren't jumping to conclusions because you don't like Violet?"

I bit my bottom lip and considered what Hitch had just said. "It all makes sense, doesn't it?"

"It does, but you could probably put together a similar scenario for Laura or Carla, or Greg, and maybe even Ashley. Or, me. Think about it, Sunny. Without *evidence*, it's all just speculation."

Hitch was right, of course. We needed evidence." I opened the car door. "Uh-oh," I said as I slid out with the casserole.

"What now?" He looked at me, puzzled.

"The lights are on in my house. You know what that means, don't you?"

"Quick! Get back in the car. I'll keep driving."

As tempting as that sounded, I knew Hitch was joking. Tilly was inside waiting for us, and there was no sense in putting off the inevitable. Besides, I was starving and couldn't wait to dig into Dani's lobster mac and cheese.

"Come on Jasper. Let's get this show on the road. You're probably hungry, too. But you won't get any of this casserole."

She jumped out and ran to the side of my house to her doggie door. She preferred letting herself in instead of waiting for me to open the front door for her.

I heard loud barking. And, when I say loud, Jasper's normal bark was loud, but this was her louder warning bark, more like a roar.

Hitch wasted no time getting to the front door. He never ran from a dangerous situation which was admirable and also scary.

What was going on inside?"

30

The front door flew open just as Hitch arrived with me only a step or two behind.

"Tilly?"

He stopped short, and I crashed into his back. It felt like I'd run into a wall.

At least his lightning reflexes kicked in, and he turned, caught my flailing arms, and kept me on my feet without missing a beat. "What's got Jasper all in an uproar?" he asked.

Greg appeared behind Tilly. "Your dog thought I was an intruder," he said. "But we've worked it out, right Jasper?"

Jasper pushed past both Greg and Tilly and sat at my side. "Good girl," I cooed and stroked her head. "You can never be too careful." I eyed Greg with suspicion.

"Come on in, you two," Tilly said. "We'd almost given up on you ever coming home. What took so long?"

Hitch glanced at me and sent a look that I took to mean in hindsight, *not coming to my house might have been the better choice.* I shrugged and hoped he understood that I meant, *nothing to do about that now.*

He put his arm around my shoulder, and we walked inside. Between Tilly's strange bouncy behavior and Greg's friendly demeanor I felt like a guest in my own home. Could my world turn any more upside down? Probably, was the sad truth.

"So," Tilly clapped her hands together. "Greg was just about to look through your fridge to find something to throw together for dinner."

I'm sure my eyebrows sank into a huge frown of displeasure at the idea of this person I barely knew making himself at home in my house. Much too brazen for my likes.

"He thought you probably didn't want to cook after working all day, and he says preparing a meal relaxes him," Tilly explained. "He wouldn't take no for an answer. So..." she held her hands in a helpless, what-do-you-want-me-to-do gesture.

This was not the Tilly I knew who managed to be a take charge person in any situation. Something strange was going on.

"I have a casserole from Dani so that won't be necessary," I said, glad to have something in my hands to keep me from strangling someone. Greg most likely, but right now I wasn't pleased with Tilly either.

"Tilly, how about you and Greg sit out here while I put this in the oven to heat." I needed space away from them. Fast. Without waiting for an answer, I walked to *my* kitchen and turned on the oven. Hitch followed me.

"What is going on?" he whispered. "I've never seen Tilly acting like a schoolgirl."

I handed Hitch the bottle of wine and the corkscrew. I'd already decided that we, or at least *I*, needed that glass of wine now. Forget about waiting for the casserole to heat up.

Unfortunately, Tilly had other ideas. Hitch had poured two glasses of the chardonnay when she barged into the kitchen and joined us. Thankfully, she hadn't pulled Greg along with her.

"Listen, you two," she said in a hushed voice. "You could at least try to be friendly. I'm trying to convince Greg to go to Violet's house and get back in the good graces of the roommates. You know," she grinned devilishly, "as a spy for us."

I helped myself to a generous gulp of wine before holding it toward Hitch to be topped up. "Tilly, they won't just let him waltz in after he walked out on them this morning. Carla already basically accused him of murdering Ginger."

"I think you're wrong, Sunny. That was all in the heat of the moment. Emotions were flaring." Tilly pulled out a chair, sat down, and laid out her plan. At least she sounded like herself again, which was a good sign. "After we left Shakes and Cakes, I dropped Greg off to get his car. The plan is, he'll go next door and apologize. He can say he was under a lot of stress, blah, blah, blah. It doesn't really matter what he says as long as he sounds sincere. I'm sure he can turn on his charm and trick them into letting him in. Then, he can sit back and listen to all the chatter; find out what they've been doing. He can even hint that he knows something about Ginger. They'll eat it right up. Perfect, right?"

Nothing was ever perfect, but the idea of Greg doing the snooping instead of us was appealing. "It's worth a shot," I grudgingly agreed. And, best of all, he'd be out of my house.

Tilly stood up. "Great. He bought a bottle of wine

for you, but I told him the roommates need it more." She raised her eyebrow at my own rapidly disappearing bottle but had enough sense to keep quiet. "That will loosen their tongues. Let me go send him off." She sniffed the air and inhaled deeply. "Save some of that casserole for me. It smells divine."

I thought about throwing a salad together but decided it was too much trouble. The lobster mac and cheese was plenty enough for me along with the wine.

Stash and Princess Muffin darted into the kitchen providing a welcomed distraction and a much-needed laugh. One chased the other and then they switched roles before both took a break to enjoy some of their crunchies.

"I hope the other kittens all get adopted into such good homes," Hitch said.

"Or, they'll stay in the greenhouse. I haven't heard any of them complain. They have sunshine, plants, an enclosed safe area outside, and don't forget the best nanny ever."

And right on cue, Jasper lumbered into the kitchen, sniffed each kitten, and stretched out in the middle of the floor. I had to walk around her to get to the oven when the timer went off.

"I can't wait," Hitch said, looking over my

shoulder at the bubbling casserole. "The aroma has my salivary glands working overtime."

I scooped out two big helpings, handing one plate to Hitch and taking the other to the table for myself. "Tilly can fend for herself if she's hungry, but I'm not waiting."

Hitch topped off our wine glasses, which drained the bottle. We had just enough to accompany our meal.

Our forks clicked on the plates. I hadn't realized how hungry I was, and the casserole filled me up quickly. "Delicious," I announced, not that Hitch hadn't already figured that out for himself.

"I wonder what's taking Tilly so long with her send-off," he said.

"I'll check." I put my fork down and slid my chair back. "Don't sneak the rest of the lobster out of the casserole," I said, watching him eye a big piece of claw meat.

"That never crossed my mind," he laughed, and I knew it was a lie.

"Hey, Tilly," I said as I walked into the living room.

Silence.

My stomach dropped.

Where did she go?

31

"Both Tilly and Greg are gone. That wasn't the plan," I said to Hitch who'd just finished his lobster mac and cheese.

A door slammed nearby.

Jasper shot out through her doggie door.

"What should we do?" I asked.

"Don't panic," Hitch said, which was like telling someone not to sneeze. It's not like I chose to panic but telling my heart to slow down was pointless.

"Come on." He reached for my hand. "Jasper is probably already on Tilly's trail."

I grabbed a flashlight from my utility drawer and followed Hitch into the backyard. He inched along my fence until we were almost to the point where we could see into Violet's yard when a car pulled into my driveway.

"Who's that?" I asked, flattening myself against the fence.

"It looks like Ashley's car."

"You told her you'd be at *my* house?" She was the last person I wanted to see tonight.

"I might have let that slip," he said sheepishly. "Wait here. I'll get rid of her."

A nail in the fence jabbed into my shoulder blade. I wiggled away and tried to calm my racing heart. It didn't work. Forcing myself to forget about Ashley, I crept a bit farther along the fence and peeked into Violet's yard.

A hand clamped over my mouth and forced me back into the shadows. "It's me, Tilly. Don't scream." She lowered her hand.

"What was that all about? You scared me half to death, and I almost wet myself." Okay, I should have kept that last bit of information to myself. Jasper walked around the fence and sat next to me. That was probably the best thing that could have happened right now.

Tilly laughed and leaned against the fence, until we were shoulder to shoulder.

I started to giggle, too. Not that the whole situation was funny, but in a way, it was and laughing helped to rid myself of some adrenaline.

"Greg is on the inside," Tilly said, like we were in some kind of undercover operation. "Carla met him in the living room and gave him a big weepy hug, I watched from the front porch and peeked through Violet's window. I think they swallowed his story hook, line, and sinker."

"Are you sure you can *trust* him?" I asked.

"Of course not, but he's the best we've got for getting any information."

The murmur of a conversation reached us.

"Who's Hitch talking to?" She shaded her eyes like that would help in this almost pitch darkness.

"Ashley showed up. I'm sure she just wanted an excuse to see him."

While we hid in the shadows, everyone walked out of Violet's house. Laura hugged her and followed Greg and Carla who strolled toward his car hand in hand. Violet waved until they'd all driven out of sight. She wiped her brow, smiled, and disappeared back inside.

"So much for your undercover spy," I said to Tilly. "It looks like he's ditched you for his wife."

"Perfect. That was my plan the whole time."

Now, I was confused.

"Laura, Carla, and Greg are all at the Bayside Bed and Breakfast. With Violet alone, my plan is to search her house after she's asleep. Are you with me on this?"

What could I do? Send her in alone? "I'm in."

She took my hand and pulled me toward my back door. "Come on. We've got some work to do."

Following Tilly's logic was difficult on a low drama day but now? My brain hurt.

My tea kettle whistled when we stepped inside. A nice cup of soothing chamomile tea might be nice right about now I told myself, until I spotted Ashley sitting at my kitchen table.

"Ashley thought she heard someone inside my apartment earlier. After the police left," Hitch said.

"That's right. I was so scared I just huddled in my corner for, like, at least an hour. I'm positive someone was in Hitch's kitchen. I heard footsteps and drawers opening and closing. It, like, really freaked me out."

I shot a look at Hitch. Was he buying this? "Did you look out your windows for cars on the street? Or anyone walking out of Hitch's place? Did you see *anything*, Ashley?"

She shook her head. "I didn't dare go close to a window. I didn't want that person to know I was home. I waited for, like forever before I dared to get in my car and come here. Please let me stay."

She looked at me with the biggest frightened eyes I'd ever seen. I couldn't believe it was an act. "Sure. You can stay. With Hitch and Jasper here, no one will dare break in."

I poured tea for everyone, and we moved into the living room. Now we had to wait for Violet's house to go dark.

"Cute place ya got here," Ashley said as she looked around.

"Thanks."

One of the kittens jumped on her lap. "Oh! Where'd you come from?" She laughed and stroked Stash until she settled on Ashley's lap. "You really like animals, don't you?"

"I do. How about you?" I asked.

"Well, it's a long story."

Oh boy, now I was sorry I'd asked.

"But the short version is that my parents wouldn't let me have a pet. I'd like to give a cat a try. I think it would be a good companion, quiet, and they're clean. What do you think?" She looked at me like I was the expert.

"It's a lifelong commitment, Ashley. Having a pet isn't just a whim until you decide it's not as much fun as you'd expected." Why mince words? "Can you commit to something like that?"

"Of course, I can. It's not like I'm irresponsible. I like, have a job, I'm always on time with paying my bills. I might need a little help since taking care of animals is new for me, but I don't think that disqualifies me." She had a good point. There was always a first time for every pet owner.

"I have an idea, Ashley."

She leaned toward me.

"We," I indicated Hitch and myself, "need someone to help out in our Kitty Castle. All of our kittens are looking for good homes. If you want to volunteer, you could get some experience. What do you think?"

Her eyes lit up. "Really? You'd trust me to, like, help? My parents never had any confidence in me."

Okay, now I felt sorry for her and took back all my original assumptions. She was sort of pathetic, but at least she was trying to improve herself.

"Sure. You'd actually be working alongside Jasper. She's our official Chief Kitty Nanny, but, obviously, she can't talk to potential adopters or help fill out the adoption application."

"I have Fridays off, so I could, like, come in for the whole day." Her eyes shone with excitement.

Hitch patted my leg to let me know he was glad I'd decided to take a chance with Ashley. "We'd love that," he said.

Tilly finished her tea and stood up. Distracted. I doubted she'd been paying any attention to the conversation with Ashley. "I need to get something from my house. Can you help me, Sunny? It might take a while."

Hitch sent me a what-are-you-two-up-to look, but I ignored him, knowing he wouldn't like whatever Tilly's plan was.

"Sure." I stood up. "Hitch, can you get sheets and blankets out of the closet and fix up the guest room for Ashley? I guess you'll have to sleep on the couch."

He followed me to the door. He wasn't going to let us leave without some kind of explanation.

"Just a little peek in Violet's windows," Tilly said. "Nothing to worry about."

"There's always something to worry about if you're involved, Tilly." Hitch said. There was an unmistakable hint of frustration and possibly worry in his tone. "I'll get Ashley settled. If you two aren't back in a half hour, I'm coming out looking for you."

That was a bit of reassurance, but I still regretted telling Tilly I'd be her partner in crime tonight.

32

After Tilly changed into a black jogging outfit and gave me her dark blue one to wear, we silently slipped out of her house.

"What are we looking for?" I whispered.

"We'll know when we find it," Tilly said as she crept across the street to Violet's yard.

I stayed behind Tilly, with one hand on her back, as we hunched over and darted from shadow to shadow. A dog barked, and we froze until the owner called the dog back inside and silence fell on our street again.

Silent except for my pounding heart. Would that give me away?

Tilly followed Violet's path to her backyard.

In the dark, I missed the edge of the path and

stepped into Violet's garden. Worried that I'd crushed one of her plants, I turned on my flashlight and checked for damage.

"What are you doing?" Tilly hissed at me. "Turn that off."

"Wait," I said. "Look at this." I pointed to holes in Violet's flower bed where something had been removed. I reached down and picked up a couple of stems covered with beautiful blue-hooded flowers. "Do you think she'll miss these?" I asked.

"Really, Sunny? You're picking posies while we're trying to gather evidence?"

"Who's there?" Violet's voice boomed from her back door. I froze, except for my racing heart, and thanked my lucky stars that we were hidden in the darkness.

Until she turned her backyard light on.

"Tilly? Sunny? You're lucky I'm tired, otherwise I'd call the police. Get off my property. Now!"

I grabbed Tilly by her arm and pulled her along with me before she had time to do something to make the situation worse.

She slapped at my hand. "Let me go, Sunny!"

When we were safely off Violet's property, I released my hold. She huffed and puffed but followed me without a word.

Jasper charged from the back of my house, on a mission to protect us if her bark meant anything.

"Shush, Jasper," I said patting her to let her know we were okay. "We don't want to give Violet another excuse to call the police."

"Call the police?" Hitch asked as he arrived just behind Jasper. "I saw the floodlight come on and heard Violet yelling. It only took you ten minutes to get into trouble? What happened?"

"Let's go inside, and I'll tell you about our adventure."

"That Sunny cut short," Tilly added. "We had the perfect opportunity to get inside Violet's house, but no, Sunny pulled me back here." She folded her arms over her chest and pouted.

"Get in her house? Are you kidding me, Tilly?" I screeched. "She was about to call the police because we were trespassing."

"Oh, she's all bluster," Tilly said, dismissing me with a wave of her hand. "I could have talked my way inside, Sunny. Now, we can't get that look-see that might have turned up a clue or two."

At this point, all I could do was shake my head. "Listen, Tilly. I'm sorry I spoiled your plans. I was trying to keep us out of jail for the night."

"Okay, I'll admit that was a possibility. But still, now we'll never know."

"Thankfully," Hitch said as he ushered us toward my house.

"Let's go inside and figure out a new plan," Tilly said. "The night is still young."

Unbelievable but there was something to be said about Tilly's ability to swerve from one dangerous predicament to another in the blink of an eye. Reckless?

Me? I had to sit down and get my nerves calmed down, which would take the rest of the night.

I dropped onto my couch, happy to have Stash and Princess Muffin join me. Jasper leaned against my legs. All that four-legged love was just the distraction I needed.

"What's that blue stuff sticking out of your pocket?" Hitch asked.

"This?" I held up the flower stem I'd picked up in Violet's garden. "I sort of fell into a hole and when I turned my flashlight on, I saw these. Pretty, aren't they? Do you know what kind of flower it is?" I handed the stem to Hitch.

"This was in Violet's yard?"

"Yeah, why?"

"This is aconitum, or monkshood, and it's very poisonous," Hitch said.

Tilly and I looked at each other. Her mouth dropped open, and I felt mine do the same.

"The clue you said we'd know when we saw it," I said to Tilly.

She leaped out of the chair. "We have to go back and get a better look in her flower patch. Are you coming?"

Hitch gently pushed her back into the chair. "Not. Tonight. Tilly. We'll look tomorrow, when it's light out. We don't even know if Ginger was poisoned. I said it was a *possibility* when I found her."

"But—"

"No, but," Hitch said with a finality that left no room for argument. "*If* it's confirmed that Ginger was poisoned like I suggested, and *if* that poison is aconitum, *then* Violet has some questions to answer. I'm not a believer in jumping to a conclusion that could destroy someone if it turns out to be false. I'm sure she's not the only gardener around who has monkshood growing in her yard."

Hitch might have a point, but I wasn't planning to turn my back on my neighbor.

33

It was strange trying to sleep with Ashley in my guest room and Hitch on the couch. Plus, the knowledge that my neighbor might have poisoned her friend with a common garden plant turned out to be more unsettling than I'd expected.

At least Jasper and my two kittens provided a humorous distraction in the morning.

I couldn't help but laugh when I walked into my living room. Hitch groaned as the kittens chased each other back and forth on top of his chest while he tried to catch last bit of shuteye before his alarm went off.

Jasper stuck her wet nose under Hitch's pillow and flipped it to the floor.

Hitch opened his eyes and stretched his arms over his head. "I see why you don't use an alarm clock, Sunshine. Is it really time to get up?"

"I'll take Jasper out if you want to stay put so the kittens can continue their game. Or, have a pot of coffee ready for when I get back?" I raised an eyebrow wondering what he'd choose.

"Hmm. I'll have to think about those choices. And when will Tilly barge in with her latest plan?" he asked.

"Sooner rather than later." I patted my leg and jiggled Jasper's leash. "Come on, Jas, ready for your walk?"

Outside, a fresh breeze from Misty Harbor brought the salty air to my nose, reminding me why I loved this area so much.

As we started walking, something caught Jasper's attention when we approached Violet's flower bed. I looked at her house and saw her peeking at me. I shivered at that penetrating stare. Fortunately, Jasper barely slowed down, gave a quick sniff at something, and then trotted past. When we got to the turnoff for the wooded path, she paused and looked at the route we normally took but stayed at my side.

A door closed. I glanced behind us and hurried straight ahead.

Chickadees flitted in the trees along the road and a flash of blue streaked overhead. The blue jay squawked his alarm that intruders were coming.

"What do you think, Jasper? Isn't it nice to stroll out here while the rest of the world is waking up?" I tried my best to bury my fear that Violet was following me.

Jasper woofed and pulled against the leash when she spotted someone heading toward us. I felt trapped between what might be behind me and who was approaching from ahead. Jasper dragged me forward.

"Sunny?" Greg waved at me.

Well this was a surprise. "Greg? Is everything alright? What are you doing out walking this morning?"

Jasper sat and insisted on an ear rub.

"That police officer contacted Carla at the bed and breakfast this morning. She'd asked him to let us know any details about Ginger's case."

He meant Officer Walker. "And?"

Greg inhaled and looked up at the sky. "He confirmed that she was poisoned."

I didn't know how to respond.

He shifted his travel mug from one hand to the other. "Yeah, Carla is with Laura. They're both a mess. They asked me to let Violet know. So," he lifted both shoulders, "here I am, walking around trying to figure out how to tell her."

"Tell Violet?" I asked. Our discovery of poisonous monkshood in her garden flashed through my brain. "Shouldn't the police be the ones to notify her?"

"That's exactly what *I* said, but, no, Carla insisted she'd take it better from me."

"I really think you should let the police handle it, Greg."

"Why? You seem kind of agitated, Sunny. Are you feeling alright?" He stepped closer and put his hand on my arm.

I wiped sweat off my brow. "I need to get home. I left without coffee or even a drink of water, and I'm feeling a little light-headed."

"Here, take a sip of this. I made it for Violet, but it looks like you need some fluids."

"What is it?"

"Actually, I planned to tell you and Hitch about my concoction with blueberries and ginger in case you want to add it to your smoothie selection." He held it toward me. "Try it."

I took the mug and lifted the cover. The drink overpowered me with the smell of ginger. I really didn't want any, but I didn't want to hurt his feelings. "What's this floating on top?"

Greg looked in the mug. "Oh, blueberries that didn't get completely blended I think." He adjusted his sunglasses and wiped sweat off his upper lip.

Why was he staring at me?

Jasper paced around me, whining. As I lifted the mug to my lips, she jumped up and pawed at my arm. The mug flew from my grip and spilled on the sidewalk.

I looked at the blue mess spreading out. Small chunks of something dark, definitely not blueberries, were mixed in the glop.

"What's wrong with your dog?" Greg shouted. He crouched down and tried to push the drink back into the mug. Was he still planning to drink this dirty mixture?

When I looked down at him again, I noticed specks of blue stuck on his sleeve. The blue contrasted dramatically with the white of his shirt.

He suddenly stood up.

I reached toward one of the specks but he grabbed my wrist.

Jasper growled.

"Call your dog off, Sunny, or I'll break your arm," Greg said.

"It *was* you." Everything became crystal clear as I saw the menace in his eyes. "You killed Ginger because she didn't want anything to do with you. You dug up the monkshood in Violet's garden."

Greg sneered as he twisted my arm behind my back and hissed his words right in my ear. "What? You thought Violet killed the special Ms. Ginger? I'm glad that's what you think because that's what everyone will believe soon enough. Poor Violet. When the police show up and find a nice mixture of blueberry, ginger, and poison hidden in her refrigerator. You and Tilly made it too easy for me last night. This drink was a spare. Just in case I ran into a problem. Like you."

He reached down and picked up a chunk of the monkshood root. "Open up, Sunny. It won't take long."

Greg jammed the hunk of root against my lips.

I clamped my mouth closed and twisted away.

I jerked my head around as I tried to get away from him.

Jasper pushed between us, but Greg tightened his grip on my arm and kept trying to force the root into my mouth. Once my lips began to tingle, self-preservation kicked into high gear. I stomped on his foot, then kneed him.

Greg yipped like a little girl but still managed to hold on to me. I couldn't get away from him.

Jasper bumped me, pushing me right up against Greg.

But, as if an invisible force intervened, my arm miraculously fell free. Greg screamed and fell on the sidewalk, writhing face-first in his poisonous concoction.

When I looked up, Ashley stood over my assailant like a warrior from out of the blue.

"Ashley?" I shook my wrist, trying to get feeling back. "Where did you come from?"

"I always, like, you know, run in the morning and ever since I saw this creep," she gave Greg a jab with her foot, "I decided I needed to carry my Taser with me at all times. Lucky for you I came this way."

Hitch's Camaro screeched to a stop next to us and a police car arrived seconds later.

"Yeah, I called Hitch when I saw that creep talking to you. You can, like, never be too careful, right? Are you okay now?"

I looked down at Greg immobilized on the ground. Yeah, with him out of commission, I was. I could tell the concern in Ashley's voice was genuine. I couldn't help but wrap my arms around her.

Hitch and Tilly bolted out of the car, adding

their hugs to Ashley's, which made for a big cluster of bodies with Jasper still glued to my side.

Police Chief Bullock limped over. He looked at Ashley holding her Taser and Greg on the ground. "What happened?"

And then I remembered Violet.

I filled him in quickly and added, "He left a poisoned drink at Violet's house. You have to warn her."

Tilly moved off to one side and made the call. All I heard was, "Don't drink anything until we get there. Trust me, Violet; this is not a joke. I'm deadly serious."

I told the Chief what I knew about Greg's plans, having trouble believing it myself.

"And, there's the evidence." I pointed to the drink on the ground. "Test it, especially those chunks. And he has bits of monkshood flower on his shirt. I guess he got careless."

The Chief hauled Greg off to the Pineville jail. Tilly, Jasper, and I barely squeezed into Hitch's car, but we didn't have far to go back to my house, and we managed. Ashley said she'd finish her run and be back soon.

"So, Ashley?" Hitch said while I was jammed

next to Tilly in the front of his car. "Bet you never thought Ashley could even rescue herself."

"Where did that bravery come from?" I asked.

"I gave her a pep talk this morning when she got up and found me in the kitchen. I was making a pot of coffee and we talked. I told her she could live in fear or she could take charge and stand up for herself. I said, it's all in your head. And you know what she told me?"

"Of course not, Hitch. I'm sure it was profound, though." Now my mind was on that pot of coffee.

"She said, and I swear these are her exact words. 'I have to, like, channel Sunny or something? I can do that.'"

I choked. "She thinks I'm some kind of superhero?"

Hitch chuckled and added, "That's what it sounded like. I think you've got a new friend, Sunshine. He patted my thigh. "You are pretty special in my book, too."

Tilly laughed until it turned into a series of snorts. "Who would have ever predicted this?"

Not me in a million years. But here I was, safe with Hitch, Tilly, and Jasper. I'd gained new respect for someone who seemed a bit ditzy at best. Boy, was I wrong.

I had a lot to learn but I planned to enjoy the ride.

In Pineville, Sunny Shaw stumbles into one sweet disaster after another!

CLICK HERE to begin *Tabby Trouble*, the next mouth watering Blueberry Bay mystery!

WHAT'S NEXT?

I'm Sunny Shaw and, lately, trouble is my middle name.

Things are close to normal again when someone dumps a tiny box of kittens in my lap. I figure I'll get them back to their mother and go about my business. No harm, no foul.

Except, I never expected to stumble over a body. Nor did I think a ten-year-old girl would be the only witness to the murder. Even worse? There's a rare bird worth a fortune somehow mixed up in this mess.

Ruffling a few feathers is the least of my worries, especially since my goose might get cooked if I don't hurry up and solve this case.

Come on, Jasper. We have kittens to take care of,

a little girl to protect, and a killer on the loose. Surviving this one will take all of our smarts.

Tabby Trouble is now available.

CLICK HERE to get your copy so that you can keep reading this series today!

SNEAK PEEK OF TABBY TROUBLE

I crouched down in the dusty driveway of my donut vendor, A Donut A Day. The clang of lobster buoys, and the squawk of seagulls barely audible in the distance.

Isabella Golden, my friend's ten-year-old daughter, stood in front of me cradling a beat up old cardboard box in her arms. She carefully held it toward me with a plea in her eyes. I opened the top flap, peeked inside, and my stomach twisted into an angry knot at the sight of three tiny tabby kittens inside. Without a word, her big blue eyes begged me to help.

I tucked a few flyaway hairs behind her ear and took the box from her dirty hands. What on earth had she been up to this early in the morning?

"Where did you find this?" I asked, ready to tear into a thoughtless owner who'd abandoned the newborns.

Her messy pigtails danced back and forth across her chest as she scuffed her well-worn sneaker in the dirt. She stared at the depression under her sneaker, avoiding my gaze.

And then she bolted. Two long, blonde pigtails flew behind her as she pumped her arms and ran down the driveway.

"Izzy! Wait!" I yelled. A salty breeze from Blueberry Bay was all that remained after she'd disappeared around the corner.

Welcome to Pineville, Maine, I reminded myself. Where the unexpected has become my new normal in this small coastal town that survives by catering to tourists. A cluster of small souvenir-filled shops, neighboring gift emporiums, and one of a kind craft stores lined Main Street. After shopping, the visitors relaxed and refueled at my business, Shakes and Cakes, with a delicious shake and sweet treat. At least, I hoped that was part of their destination.

"What was *that* all about, Sunny?" Tilly, my seventy-year-old neighbor, friend, and enthusiastic helper at Shakes and Cakes asked as she stared down the driveway. She'd just finished loading my donut order in the back seat of her chili pepper-red VW bug.

Tilly Morris, not one to fluster easily, peered over my shoulder into the box. Her colorful scarf fluttered around her short gray hair.

"Oh, my lord. At least their eyes are open. Do you think they're even three weeks old yet?"

Tilly's choked-up voice and misty eyes were a stark contrast to the nothing-bothers-me persona that she usually wore. "We might have to bottle feed them, you know."

As if I had no clue about kittens.

Tilly had a point, of course, but first I had to find out where they'd come from. Maybe the mother cat was still around, which would be the ideal solution. But until I found her, if I *could* find her, the little darlings needed a clean space and possibly a bottle every three to four hours. I wondered how I'd manage a schedule like that for these three tiny tabby kittens while also serving customers at Shakes and Cakes.

To be clear, I had a business partner. Even though Ty Hitchner had financed the whole operation, I was an equal partner. But I was determined to pay my fair share eventually. And, he'd never blinked an eye when I suggested we turn the attached greenhouse of the previous old nursery business into a kitty jungle for strays. The combination of shakes, cakes, and kittens had already become a major attraction here in Pineville, Maine, on beautiful Blueberry Bay. I mean, who *wouldn't* love to relax amidst a tropical-like jungle with an exotic shake in one hand and a kitten or two in your lap?

You've got to love a guy like Hitch whose heart is bigger than the moon when it comes to kittens in need. And, I reminded myself, it didn't hurt that he had those heart-stopping sea green eyes, a chiseled chin, and dimples when he smiled. But that was a whole different story. One I didn't have time to dwell on at the moment.

"What will Hitch say about this?" Tilly asked. Apparently, we thought alike as she mentioned the very same person I had on my mind.

"We'll find out soon enough. He's already at Shakes and Cakes getting all the ingredients chopped, labeled, and organized for our breakfast smoothies." Our task was picking up the donuts. I hadn't dreamed I'd be bringing more than our regular order back to the shop. I took another look at the kittens and my heart about melted from the cuteness.

Before we'd even stepped away from the doorway of A Donut A Day, the owner, driving her white delivery van, rolled into the driveway and pulled up in front of us.

"Morning," Ruby Todd said as she slid from the driver seat. She adjusted her old lady reading glasses (not that she was old, only mid-forties) on top of her head to hold her curly hair in place.

"I hope you found your donut order without any trouble. I would have been here sooner to help, but boy oh boy, what a morning I've had," she said, And not in a good way. The morning sun picked up a few brassy glints in the new shade of red she sported this week.

"We found the donut order without any trouble," I said. "But look at *this* surprise Isabella brought over. I certainly wasn't expecting anything like this in addition to your dozens of donuts today." I hoped my tone wasn't harsh, but my day hadn't started well either.

"Jessica's daughter? That little scallywag was supposed to wait next door for me to get back from my delivery. Jess called me in a panic when she couldn't find Izzy this morning. She had to get to her dog walking job, so I offered to look for the little imp and found her at the end of Ron Silva's driveway." Ruby rolled her eyes. "What did she do? Dump the kittens here and run? By any chance, did she tell you where she was going?"

"Nope. She took off like she was running the fifty-yard dash, and yes, she left this box of kittens."

"I hope she's headed back next door. Jess is housesitting there." Ruby glanced at her watch. "Jess won't be back until she finishes her dog walking job." She reached for the box with the kittens. "Let me take a look at the little fur balls."

When Ruby took the box from me, faint mews came from inside. Her expression softened as soon as she peeked in the box. She wrinkled her brow, showing concern. "They're so tiny."

"Three teeny tiny tabbies, Ruby. Izzy took off when I asked her where they came from."

"I know exactly where they came from. Izzy left a note for Jess that she was riding her bike to Ron's barn even though she *knows* she's not allowed. Izzy and Ron struck up quite the friendship when Jess was dating him, and now Izzy sneaks over on a regular basis, completely ignoring her mother's rule. She wouldn't tell me why she took the kittens, though. Want me to take them back to Ron?"

The kittens mewed pathetically, which practically broke my heart.

"These little fur balls are hungry." I formulated a plan as I walked over to Tilly's car. "I'll take them to my Kitty Castle, feed them, and make them comfortable. Ruby, you track Izzy down and bring her to Shakes and Cakes. Bribe her with her favorite milkshake and cupcake if you have to. No ten-year-old can resist that," I said, hoping I was right. I wanted to have as much information as possible about the kittens before I dropped in on Ron to accuse him of being irresponsible. I hoped that wasn't true.

"Sure, Sunny. If she's where she should be, I'll say this is my lucky day and you'll see us in thirty minutes. I love that kid to pieces, but I don't envy Jess. Izzy is smart, stubborn, and pushes every limit there is. And it's worse since Jess broke up with Ron because of that guy that's been staying in his barn."

That description of Izzy, especially the stubborn part, reminded me of someone *I* knew who drove a chili pepper-red VW bug, but I wasn't naming any names.

"Perfect." I slid onto the passenger seat of Tilly's bug. I'd just reached up to tuck some stray hairs into my French braids when she hit the gas. "Whoa!" I held onto the box of kittens with both hands and hoped my seatbelt was tight enough. "Be careful. We've got all the boxes of donuts in the back plus these babes."

"Oh, right. I was only thinking of getting the kittens to the Kitty Castle as quickly as possible," Tilly said. "Do you think someone dumped them and Izzy just happened to stumble on that box?"

"I don't know, Tilly. Ruby said they came from Ron's barn. Let's wait to hear what Izzy has to say for herself."

"If she's not at Shakes and Cakes in a half hour, I'm going to talk to Ron myself," Tilly said with that don't argue with me tone.

Great. Now, I had to worry about Tilly, angry and going off half-cocked. "Let me know before you do that," I said.

Tilly glanced at me and grinned. "I knew you'd see it my way."

"Watch out!"

Tilly swerved back into her lane and laughed. "Isn't life exciting?"

That wasn't exactly how I'd describe spending time with Tilly Morris. It was more like trying to outswim a white shark with an anchor tied around my ankle... always on the verge of drowning under one problem or another.

What the heck was in store for me today?

What happens next?
Don't wait to find out...

CLICK HERE to get your copy so that you can keep reading this zany mystery series today!

MORE BLUEBERRY BAY

We hope you enjoyed your visit to Blueberry Bay, a scenic region of Maine peppered with quaint small towns and home to a shocking number of mysteries. If you loved this book, then make sure to check out its sister series from other talented Cozy Mystery authors...

Visit SweetPromisePress.com/BlueberryBay to pick your next read!

But wait, there's more! If you loved this book, we're pretty sure you're just the kind of reader Sweet Promise Press is looking for!

Each of our books is guaranteed clean, wholesome, and happy. Some of our best-selling series include:

- *Pet Whisperer P.I. (Cozy Mystery)*
- *Gold Coast Retrievers (Romantic Suspense)*
- *Holidays in Hallbrook (Contemporary Romance)*
- *Secret Academy (Paranormal)*
- *Pioneer Brides of Rattlesnake Ridge (Historical Romance)*
- *... and there's so much more to discover!*

No matter what your reading mood, we're pretty sure we have something that fits.

Check out the links below to learn more and to connect with our talented team of authors and enthusiastic community of readers.

Browse our books by genre:
sweetpromisepress.com/Library

Download our free app:
sweetpromisepress.com/App

Join our Facebook group:
sweetpromisepress.com/Group

Sign up for our newsletter:

sweetpromisepress.com/Subscribe

Like us on Facebook:
sweetpromisepress.com/FB

MORE SWEET PROMISE PRESS

If you loved this book, we're pretty sure you're just the kind of reader Sweet Promise Press is looking for!

Each of our books is guaranteed clean, wholesome, and happy. Some of our best-selling series include:

- *Pet Whisperer P.I. (Cozy Mystery)*
- *Gold Coast Retrievers (Romantic Suspense)*
- *Holidays in Hallbrook (Contemporary Romance)*
- *Secret Academy (Paranormal)*
- *Pioneer Brides of Rattlesnake Ridge (Historical Romance)*
- *... and there's so much more to discover!*

No matter what your reading mood, we're pretty sure we have something that fits.

Check out the links below to learn more and to connect with our talented team of authors and enthusiastic community of readers.

Browse our books by genre:

sweetpromisepress.com/Library

Download our free app:

sweetpromisepress.com/App

Join our Facebook group:

sweetpromisepress.com/Group

Sign up for our newsletter:

sweetpromisepress.com/Subscribe

Like us on Facebook:

sweetpromisepress.com/FB

MORE EMMIE!

I hope you enjoyed this book.

Click here to sign up for my newsletter and never miss a new release.

About Emmie Lyn

Emmie Lyn shares her world with her husband, a rescue terrier named Underdog, and a black cat named Ziggy. When she's not busy thinking of ways to kill off a character, she loves enjoying tea and chocolate in her flower garden, hiking, or spending time near the ocean.

Emmielynbooks.com

More from Emmie

COZY MYSTERIES

Little Dog Diner Cozy Mystery Series

[Mixing Up Murder](#)

[Serving Up Suspects](#)

[Dishing Up Deceit](#)

[Cooking Up Chaos](#)

[Crumbling Up Crooks](#)

[Dicing Up Disaster](#)

[Mint Chocolate Chip Mysteries](#)

Claws of Justice

Ginger Danger

Tabby Trouble

Tuxedo Bravado

Furrgone Conclusion

Romantic Suspense

[Gold Coast Retriever Series](#)

[Helping Hanna](#)

[Shielding Shelly](#)